THE SINS OF LADY DACEY

THE SINS OF LADY DACEY

Marion Chesney

Chivers Press
Bath, Avon, England

Thorndike Press
Thorndike, Maine USA

This Large Print edition is published by Chivers Press, England, and by Thorndike Press, USA.

Published in 1995 in the U.K. by arrangement with the author.

Published in 1995 in the U.S. by arrangement with Ballantine Books, a division of Random House, Inc.

U.K. Hardcover ISBN 0–7451–2959–5 (Chivers Large Print)
U.K. Softcover ISBN 0–7451–2969–2 (Camden Large Print)
U.S. Softcover ISBN 0–7862–0302–1 (General Series Edition)

The text of this Large Print edition is unabridged.
Other aspects of the book may vary from the original edition.

Set in 16 pt. New Times Roman.

Printed in Great Britain on acid-free paper.

British Library Cataloguing in Publication Data available

Library of Congress Cataloging-in-Publication Data

Chesney, Marion.
The sins of Lady Dacey / Marion Chesney.
p. cm.
ISBN 0–7862–0302–1 (lg. print : lsc)
1. Large type books. I. Title.
[PR6053.H4535S565 1994]
823′.914—dc20 94–19729

CHAPTER ONE

Honoria Goodham was in church as usual. At the age of eighteen, she sometimes felt that most of her young life had been spent on her knees in church. Her parents were very religious. She had been with them to matins, and now it was evensong with the dark night shrouding the village outside and the wind whistling mournfully down from the Yorkshire moors and making the tall candles on the altar flicker and dance. Shadows like the demons that had just entered Honoria's life danced up the lime-washed walls of the old building.

The vicar intoned the words of the twelfth psalm, and the words wound in and out of her troubled brain.

'Help me, Lord, for there is not one godly man left: for the faithful are minished from among the children of men.

'They talk of vanity every one with his neighbour: they do but flatter with their lips and dissemble in their double heart.'

Her parents surely had double hearts and were possessed of vanity, thought Honoria miserably.

Her mind slid back to that morning after matins. She could see her parents seated comfortably in front of a small fire in the drawing room, placid and sure as ever, her mother with her grey hair piled up under a muslin cap and her twinkling humorous eyes which belied the fact that she had no sense of humour at all, and her father, thin and bent, cracking his knuckles in that irritating way he had and announcing that a marriage had been arranged for her.

Her thoughts had quickly ranged over the eligible young men of the neighbourhood. Perhaps it was young Mr Lance of the merry blue eyes and fair hair.

And then the blow had fallen. 'You are to wed Mr Pomfret.'

Mr Pomfret was a mill owner of forty years, a widower reported to have bullied his wife into her grave, coarse and fat and vulgar.

To Honoria's shocked protests, she was told that Mr Pomfret was very wealthy and it was her duty to marry the man chosen for her.

It was hard to break the pattern of eighteen years of dutiful obedience. But now, as the psalm finished and she knelt in prayer, Honoria clasped her hands and wondered if God really existed. What had she ever done in all her blameless life that such a marriage should have been arranged for her?

Sheltered by the high wooden walls of the family pew, she was spared the sight of Mr Pomfret, but she knew he was in the pew behind and she felt she could sense his thick body waiting for her.

'Lighten our darkness, we beseech you, O Lord,' the congregation prayed, 'and by thy great mercy defend us from all perils and dangers of this night . . .'

Her lips moving soundlessly, Honoria prayed with all her heart and soul. 'I do not want to marry Mr Pomfret. Save me from him!'

But as she walked from the cold church with her parents, there was Mr Pomfret standing in the porch with the vicar.

He leered at Honoria and then gave Mr Goodham a vulgar wink. 'I shall be calling on you tomorrow afternoon to arrange that . . . er . . . business.'

'Sound man,' commented her father, as they walked to their carriage through the slanting gravestones.

'I wish I were under one of those gravestones right now,' said Honoria, clearly and passionately.

'Hush. Fie! For shame. People will hear you!' exclaimed her mother. One parent on either side of her like jailors, they hustled her to the carriage.

'Not a word more,' admonished her mother. 'We will talk to you when we reach the privacy of our own home.'

Tears blinded Honoria's eyes as the carriage rolled home in the darkness.

'Now,' said Mrs Goodham when they had removed their wraps and were seated in the drawing room among the forbidding black Jacobean furniture, 'we will make a certain allowance for bride nerves, but do not ever be so unmaidenly, so vulgar, as to subject us to another similar outburst. Have we not given you the best governess, the best of everything? Is this how you repay us?'

Honoria clasped her hands and looked at her parents with appeal in her wide dark-blue eyes. She was still like a schoolgirl, for she had not yet been allowed to put her hair up and wore her brown hair in two long pigtails. 'Are we so poor?' she asked. 'Are we so destitute that I am to be forced into marriage with a man more than twice my age?'

'Pride goeth before a fall,' quoted her father severely. 'Pomfret may be in trade, but he is a worthy man for all that. We have sometimes been distressed by signs of flightiness in you, Honoria. You need an older man to school you.'

'To beat me into an early grave,' said Honoria bitterly.

'You are insolent!' Mrs Goodham stood up. 'Go to your room and do not leave it until you have decided to offer us a full apology. Mr Pomfret is calling tomorrow to make his proposal. You are not too old for a beating to chastise that saucy soul of yours.'

So Honoria went to her room and sat by the window, looking out into the dark night. If only she could run away. But she did not have a friend in the world. Her parents were of the gentry and considered none of the young ladies of the village suitable companions for their daughter. And yet they were prepared to force her into marriage with such a piece of vulgarity as Mr Pomfret.

A tear rolled down Honoria's small nose. She looked out and up at the dark sky where one star twinkled among the racing, ragged clouds.

'Save me,' she said simply, 'for I cannot bear it.'

* * *

Mrs Goodham enjoyed a good breakfast the following morning, untroubled by conscience. She had given birth to Honoria long after she had given up hope of bearing a healthy child. She had previously had six miscarriages. She was not by nature a maternal woman and had passed the baby immediately to a wet nurse, then a nursery maid and then a governess. The governess, a diligent if equally humourless woman, had been given her marching orders the year before. The Goodhams had begun to fear she had taught their daughter *too much*, well aware that a well-informed mind in a lady was a sore disadvantage. The governess, however, had been just as religious as the Goodhams and so Honoria had never been allowed to pollute her mind with novels.

The postboy sounded his horn and, a few moments later, the maid brought in the post bag.

'Why, there is one for you, Mrs Goodham!' exclaimed Mr Goodham. 'It has a crest.'

He opened it and started to read, it being a husband's right and duty to read his wife's letters first. 'Dear me,' he said over and over again.

Mrs Goodham waited patiently. It was a wife's duty to wait until her husband had finished reading her post.

At long last, he said, 'Bless my soul!' and handed it to her.

Mrs Goodham took the stiff parchment and read the scrawling, spidery writing. 'It is from my sister,' she said, just as if her husband had not read the letter several times.

'You did not tell me she had become Lady Dacey,' said Mr Goodham.

'And a widow now,' said Mrs Goodham, pursing her lips. 'Lady Dacey! Who would have thought it.'

She had not seen her sister, Clarissa, since Clarissa had run off with a half-pay captain all those years ago. No one ever knew what became of the captain, but Clarissa's name had appeared two years later in the social columns as having married a Colonel Phillips. Four years after that there was another wedding announcement, this time to a Mr Ward. Mrs Goodham had then given up reading the social column, as had her husband, considering the information too frivolous for sober minds.

'How old is Clarissa now?' asked Mr Goodham.

'Let me see, she ran away with that redcoat when she was sixteen. She must be all of thirty-five. But *Lady* Dacey, relict of the *Earl* of Dacey, and she wishes to *bring out* Honoria and says she could marry a duke. A duke!'

The fact that Clarissa, now Lady Dacey, had never been mentioned to Honoria because they did not want the girl to know she had such a scandalous aunt was forgotten. A title and wealth had washed all Lady Dacey's sins as white as snow in the minds of the Goodhams.

'Clarissa is, however, most insistent that we do not accompany our daughter to London,' said Mrs Goodham. 'She says we would *cramp her style*. Really! But the quality will have little foibles.' She gave an almost girlish giggle. 'Just think, Mr Goodham, our little Honoria a duchess.'

'Mr Pomfret is calling this afternoon,' pointed out Mr Goodham.

'But this changes everything. The man smells of the shop,' remarked his wife haughtily. 'You must take out the fly and drive over to The Elms and tell him that matters have changed.' She studied the letter again. 'Clarissa wants Honoria to leave as soon as possible, and we are not to bother about having clothes made for her because provincial clothes are not suitable for London.'

'Who's to pay for these London clothes?' demanded Mr Goodham.

'She will, of course!' said his wife. 'I had better tell Honoria. Mind you, she cannot travel alone all the way to London. We must find someone suitable to accompany her.'

'Mrs Perryworth, our vicar's wife, has a sister in London,' pointed out Mr Goodham, 'and she was saying t'other day that she should dearly like to pay her a visit.'

'Nothing could be more suitable.' Mrs Goodham's eyes shone. 'Call at the vicarage on your way to Pomfret's.'

* * *

The vicar's wife, Mrs Perryworth, was out walking. She was a small, dainty woman of twenty-nine. She had soft fair hair and large brown eyes. Her once full mouth was crimped in at the corners and her still excellent figure was not shown to advantage in an old-fashioned round gown of scratchy wool like a hair shirt, covered with a faded blue cloak.

She was childless. It was tacitly accepted that she was barren and the Good Lord had seen fit to make her so, but as her husband had had a distaste from day one of their marriage to the intimacies of the marriage bed, she sometimes wondered if he had been waiting for some sort of immaculate conception on her part. Her daintiness and prettiness hid the fact that she had a strong, well-educated mind. She did what she could for the parish and was grateful for the energetic help of Honoria Goodham, sometimes envying the young girl her rigid faith and delight in good works.

Mrs Pamela Perryworth often longed to hear someone call her Pamela again. Her parents were dead and her two brothers in the navy and far from home. Her husband and the parishioners called her Mrs Perryworth, as did Honoria. She often walked miles up on the moors as if to walk away her loneliness and frustration.

She eventually slowly turned her steps back toward the village. High winds were chasing torn dirty grey clouds across the sky. Rooks wheeled and cawed over the heather, tumbling about in the gale like acrobats, while a kestrel with spread wings soared majestically above them.

She thought about her sister, Amy, in London. She had not seen Amy for ten years. She had begged and pleaded to go and visit her, but her husband would say vaguely, 'Maybe next year,' and next year would come and then another without his giving his permission.

Mrs Perryworth was bored and restless. But she was used to being so, and often chastised herself for a lack of acceptance, a lack of humility.

She saw the Goodhams' horse and fly

outside the vicarage. She had heard of the proposed marriage for Honoria and disapproved of it heartily. She had begged her husband to stop the Goodhams from sacrificing Honoria, but he had listened to her in the cold, remote way he always seemed to listen to her these days and said he could not intercede between parents and daughter.

So instead of letting herself in by the front door, she went round the back of the vicarage and entered by the kitchen door and so went up the backstairs to her room, a bedroom of her own, for she had never shared a bedroom with her husband.

She sat down by the window and tried to calm her restless feelings of discontent, for the wind seemed to have got inside her very soul with its restless turbulence.

'Oh, God, am I to rot here till I die?' she cried aloud.

The door opened and her husband walked in. He was a tall man, handsome in a bloodless way. He had thick fair hair, a square face, and eyes like the North Sea, grey and cold.

'Did you call out?' he asked his wife.

'Yes, Mr Perryworth, I thought I saw a particularly large spider.'

'You must descend immediately. Mr Goodham has called. He has a most unusual request.'

Mrs Perryworth gave a little sigh but dutifully followed her husband down the stairs to the vicarage parlour. She assumed Mr Goodham had called with some request regarding the wedding arrangements.

The vicar went and took up a position in front of the fireplace. Mr Goodham sketched a bow and then said eagerly, 'Did you ask her?'

'I wish you to put the matter to Mrs Perryworth yourself,' said the vicar.

Mrs Perryworth sat down. Mr Goodham flipped up his coat-tails and sat down opposite her.

'We have received most surprising news this morning. Mrs Goodham's sister is the Dowager Countess of Dacey!'

Mrs Perryworth looked at him in surprise. Was she supposed to congratulate him?

Instead she said mildly, 'I did not know Mrs Goodham had a sister.'

'We do not often talk of family matters. Yes. Lady Dacey wishes Honoria to go to London for her come-out!'

Mrs Perryworth looked puzzled. 'I had understood a marriage was to be arranged for Honoria with Mr Pomfret.'

'Yes, yes, but naturally that is at an end. Lady Dacey says she has the best connections and that Honoria could marry a duke.'

The vicar's wife had a sudden mental picture of Honoria, with her girlish provincial gowns and her hair in two straight brown pigtails, and repressed a smile.

'Lady Dacey is most insistent that neither

myself nor Mrs Goodham go with Honoria. The aristocracy will have their little foibles,' added Mr Goodham as if marriage into the breed automatically conferred eccentricity. 'As you have a sister in London, too, Mrs Perryworth, I was hoping I could prevail on you to accompany Honoria and stay with her as chaperon.'

Hope skyrocketed inside Mrs Perryworth. London! Excitement, life, and colour.

Carefully keeping her voice neutral in case any show of enthusiasm would cause her husband to change his mind, for it was obvious he approved of the idea, she said with head bowed, 'I should consider it a privilege to escort Honoria.'

'Good, good!' The now proud father rubbed his hands. 'The other matter is a question of time. Lady Dacey is anxious for my daughter to leave as soon as possible. But if next week is too pressing . . .'

'Not at all,' said Mrs Perryworth calmly. 'I shall send an express to my sister, Amy, for I would like to see her again.'

'So that's settled,' said the vicar with a cheerfulness he did not feel. He had been flattered that his wife had been chosen to go to a countess's household. But he had never before been separated from his wife, and he suddenly wondered what it would be like to sit writing his sermons with no graceful figure moving about the room or sitting sewing quietly in the lamplight.

'What does Honoria say to this?' asked Mrs Perryworth.

'Honoria does not yet know, but she will do as she is bid,' said Mr Goodham. He refused Mrs Perryworth's offer of refreshment and took himself off to see Mr Pomfret for what he feared would be a distasteful interview.

Mrs Perryworth went up to her room. She stood for a long moment feeling joy surge through her. Freedom! She began to sing under her breath and pirouette about the room. The door swung open and her husband stood watching her. She stopped when she saw him and said with a self-conscious laugh, 'I cannot remember when I last danced. I must get in practice for my role as chaperon.'

Something flashed in his eyes and he said sharply, 'As a respectable matron it will be your duty to sit with the other chaperons. There will be no need for you to dance.'

Mrs Perryworth could hear the grating sound of the prison doors slowly beginning to close. 'Of course, you have the right of it as usual, Mr Perryworth,' she said meekly.

He studied her long and hard and then appeared satisfied. When he had left, Mrs Perryworth let out a sigh. She would go about her duties quietly and calmly. She composed herself and sat down to write an urgent letter to her sister.

* * *

Honoria walked up and down her room, wondering if she dare defy her parents and tell Mr Pomfret she would not marry him. To add to her worries, the house was strangely silent. She had not received any breakfast and that was not unusual when she was in disgrace, but what *was* unusual was the brooding silence of the house, a *waiting* silence. And then about noon, she heard the rattle of the fly as her father returned from wherever he had been and her mother's excited voice raised in greeting.

A few moments later, the key clicked in her door, for she had been locked in, and a little maid popped her head around it and said, 'Please, miss, you are to go downstairs.'

Honoria straightened her spine and stiffened her soul. She would try to plead, she would cry and beg if necessary, but she was not going to marry Mr Pomfret. She had prayed to God but He obviously thought her request for deliverance too frivolous for His attention.

When she entered the drawing room, to her surprise her mother rushed to her and hugged her, crying, 'Oh, my dear child.'

Embarrassed, Honoria detached herself from this unusual parental embrace.

'Calmly, Mrs Goodham,' said her father. 'Honoria, we have momentous news for you. You are to go to London next week to stay with your aunt, Lady Dacey.'

Honoria looked bewildered. Her speech about Mr Pomfret died stillborn on her lips.

Instead she said, 'My *aunt*?'

'My sister,' said Mrs Goodham. 'She is the Dowager Countess of Dacey and she wishes to bring you out. You will have a Season in London. Clarissa, your aunt, says you could marry a duke.'

She picked up Lady Dacey's letter and scanned it again.

Honoria's mind worked rapidly. Obviously this offer had just arrived and snobbery had defeated the pretensions of Mr Pomfret, the mill owner. So she was not even going to mention Mr Pomfret. Deliverance had arrived!

'Your aunt does not wish us to go with you.' Mrs Goodham gave a deprecatory little laugh. 'She was always given to whims and foibles, but we must indulge her as she is being so generous. But naturally we could not let you go without a chaperon. Mrs Perryworth is to accompany you.'

Honoria had always considered Mrs Perryworth a quiet, colourless woman. But it could have been worse. They could have engaged some sort of female dragon.

'I am most grateful to Mrs Perryworth,' said Honoria meekly, quickly deciding, although she did not know it, to behave like her new chaperon in a quiet and chastened way until she was free.

But she could not help asking, 'Why have I

not heard of this aunt before? I did not even know you had a sister, Mama.'

'Oh, I must have said something,' said Mrs Goodham hurriedly. 'You are such a forgetful child. But to more important things. Lady Dacey says she will furnish your clothes as what you have or can get made here will no doubt be considered sadly provincial in London. But you must be equipped for the journey.'

Despite her determination to appear calm and modest, excitement bubbled up in Honoria. 'I should at least put my hair up, Mama, for Lady Dacey will find me schoolgirlish.'

'I wish her to see you as you are,' said Mr Goodham repressively, 'pure and unsullied by vanity.'

Unlike you, thought Honoria with uncharacteristic rebellion. What is Mr Pomfret compared to a titled relative?

'Perhaps it would be a good idea if you were to pay a call on Mrs Perryworth and thank her,' said Mrs Goodham.

'Yes, of course.' But Honoria felt that sinking feeling she always had when a visit to the vicarage was suggested. The vicar was such a chilly personality, and the vicarage itself was so meanly fired that Honoria always felt cold inside and out when she went there. Still, all her young life had been glued together by duty, 'stern daughter of the voice of God,' and she went upstairs to put on her bonnet and cloak.

As the vicarage was only a short walk away, there was no reason for a maid to accompany her. Honoria hardly ever went out alone, being accompanied about the village on calls by her mother. The wind had strengthened to a gale and was tossing the bare branches of the trees up to the angry heavens. Once she was out of sight of her home, she picked up her skirts and began to run, flying before the buffeting wind, feeling she was running toward a glorious future which did not contain Mr Pomfret.

So that when she nearly collided with him, she shrank back in horror.

His heavy face was dark with anger. 'So I am to be cast aside—' he sneered '—because your mama has rediscovered that trollop of a sister.'

'How dare you speak of my aunt in such a way.' Honoria gasped.

'Because it's true. We all remember Clarissa Ward as she was, flirting and ogling the redcoats. Ran away with one o' them, didn't she? Aha! Never told you that, did they?'

'Let me pass.' Honoria looked at him haughtily.

He glanced around quickly and then gave her a slow smile. 'Reckon as I'll sample a bit of the wares that's going to Lunnon.' He reached for her but she darted back.

'Honoria!' called a sweet voice. Mr Pomfret swore under his breath and strode on as the vicar's wife came hurrying up.

'I am so glad to see you,' said Honoria. 'That man!'

'You need never see him again,' said Mrs Perryworth.

'No,' said Honoria simply, and then she began to cry.

'Come with me. What did Mr Pomfret do or say? This is dreadful. I shall get Mr Perryworth to speak to him.'

Honoria shook her head and dried her tears. 'I am crying with relief.'

Mrs Perryworth, mindful always of her husband's rigid views, said, 'Well, you must not blame your parents. They thought they were doing the best they could for you.' Honoria flashed her a disappointed look. For one moment earlier, Mrs Perryworth had seemed to come to life. Now she was once more colourless and correct.

Over the tea tray in the vicarage, Mrs Perryworth told Honoria that her sister Amy, married to a lawyer, lived in Lincoln's Inn Fields in London, and that she had not seen her for a long time. Her voice began to become animated again. Then she sprang to her feet and said with a guilty little laugh, 'I have two fashion magazines hidden in the bottom drawer of the bureau. They are five years old. Do you think fashions will have changed so very much?'

'How can I say?' Honoria laughed as well and held out the skirt of her simple girlish gown. 'I never wear anything fashionable.'

Mrs Perryworth found the magazines, and they bent their heads over the plates. 'How beautiful the ladies look!' she sighed. 'And so very tall! Do you think London ladies will all be so tall, Honoria? I shall feel like a dwarf. And surely you will now be allowed to put your hair up.'

'Papa wants me to arrive looking pure and unsullied,' said Honoria in a sudden mocking imitation of her father's rather mincing voice.

Mrs Perryworth laughed. At that moment the door opened and the vicar stood there. One of the irritating things about him, thought Honoria, as the laughter died on Mrs Perryworth's lips and her face lost all animation, was that he didn't walk into a room, he stood on the threshold in a rather intimidating way, like a stern parent looking for trouble.

He is going to ask, 'Why are you laughing?' in that reproving way he has, thought Honoria, and the vicar did just that.

'Honoria has brought me two fashion journals,' said the vicar's wife, 'and is asking my advice.'

'Indeed!' The vicar walked forward and held out an imperious hand for the journals which, having taken, he then scanned, his face registering distaste for the wordly vanities of women.

'I am surprised, Miss Goodham,' he said,

'that your parents should allow such vanities in their home.'

Honoria sensed the sudden frightened stillness inside Mrs Perryworth and in a split second knew that the vicar was probably looking for some excuse to stop his wife from going, that he already regretted having given his permission. 'I came through the village on my way here,' she said lightly, 'and was given these by Mrs Battersby. She is a frivolous lady, I admit, but very kind, and I did not like to disappoint her. Besides, as I am to have a Season, it is important to know what I am expected to wear.' And, she thought, I will now have to go through the village on the way back and call on Mrs Battersby and beg her to say she gave me the journals, for the vicar will ask her if she did. He is that kind of man. Always looking for faults.

But she was glad she had lied, for she sensed the gratitude in the vicar's wife.

'We must discuss the best way for you to travel to London,' said the vicar, dropping the journals on the table in front of them. 'Too many common people travel by the stage. I think you should travel post. I will suggest it to your father.'

He nodded to them both and left, closing the door slowly and quietly behind him. There was no sound of retreating footsteps. He is listening at the door, thought Honoria.

She raised her voice. 'We will not trouble our

heads over these fashions anymore, Mrs Perryworth. I am sure my aunt will be able to arrange everything for both of us. I have just received a vastly interesting book of sermons by the Reverend John Simms. I could pass the tedium of the journey by reading them to you, if you so wish.'

'That would be most kind of you,' said Mrs Perryworth. The footsteps at the other side of the door could then be heard retreating.

We are now conspirators and friends, thought Honoria, smiling at Mrs Perryworth. I might be going to have some fun for the first time in my life. But Honoria's religious training had been rigid, and she immediately felt wicked. As if Mrs Perryworth had had the same thought, the vicar's wife made tepid and colourless conversation for the rest of the visit.

* * *

Two days before they were due to depart, the wind, which had been roaring in from the west, suddenly veered round to the north and brought on its wings the metallic smell of threatening snow.

The villagers scanned the sky and said the roads would soon be blocked. Honoria and Mrs Perryworth began to feel frightened, knowing from experience that a bad winter might mean they would not be able to travel for weeks.

Honoria and Mrs Perryworth grew quiet and anxious. Mr Perryworth seemed to his wife to delight in saying several times a day, 'Well, my dear, it looks as if you will not be going after all.'

But the day of their departure dawned still and fair with frost glittering among the furrows of the brown winter fields.

The post chaise with its taciturn driver arrived from the nearest town. The vicarage groom and the Goodhams' groom were to ride on either side. The vicar drove his wife over to the Goodhams', his eyes occasionally cast up to the sky as if hardly able to believe that the weather had turned fine.

Both Honoria and Mrs Perryworth were wearing drab travelling dresses and cloaks and depressing bonnets, each instinctively knowing that any sign of happiness or excitement might cause the whole journey to be cancelled.

Honoria, during the days of waiting, had not mentioned Mr Pomfret's name. She had not dared ask anything about her cancelled engagement in case her parents might change their minds again and decide he was a better prospect than the risky one of her finding some noble in London.

Seated at last in the post chaise, Honoria took Mrs Perryworth's hand and held it tight. The carriage lurched forward over the frost-hard road. Mrs Perryworth waved her handkerchief to the vicar, who was standing on her side of the carriage, and Honoria, to her parents, who were on the other.

Bolt upright they both sat, staring straight ahead until the carriage climbed up the rise leading out of the village and began to traverse the wild moors.

Honoria sank back in her seat.

'It looks as if we are going to London after all, Mrs Perryworth.'

The vicar's wife smiled like a young girl. 'Pamela. Please call me Pamela.'

CHAPTER TWO

The first day of their journey was pleasant. Pamela gained new confidence from handling the money at each stop for their refreshment and change of horses. By the time they stopped for the night, both felt like world travellers, happy and confident and still buoyed up by a heady feeling of release.

The dent in their newfound confidence was caused by Honoria when she ordered a bottle of wine at supper. Pamela looked surprised, knowing that the Goodhams believed in temperance as did her own husband, but did not like to spoil the occasion with any protest. It only seemed right to join Honoria and finish the bottle and then to round off the meal with several glasses of old port.

Giggling happily, they went to bed together, Honoria, who was a good mimic, even going so far as to do a marvellous impression of the vicar's chilly, admonishing, fault-finding voice.

The room in which they slept was well-fired but close and stuffy, and both of them awoke on a bleak morning feeling decidedly ill. And when they looked out of the window, blinking painfully in the light, it was to face a steel-grey day where a cold wind was whipping tiny pellets of snow around the inn yard.

It was very hard to separate spirituality from superstition, and both were beset at the same time with a vision of a punishing God. Had they not drunk the night before, had Honoria not done her malicious impressions, had Pamela not laughed so loudly at them, then the weather would have remained fine.

So two very subdued ladies got into the post chaise, and when Pamela took out her Book of Common Prayer and began to read, Honoria asked her meekly to read aloud.

They stopped for a meal at one o'clock, and the driver and outriders confronted them and suggested they should all stay at the inn in which they found themselves, for the weather was worsening.

But Honoria and Pamela began to panic. They were not yet far enough from home. 'Just let us try a little farther,' said Honoria, and when the driver gloomily shook his head,

Pamela said sharply, 'You will continue to do what you are being paid to do.'

Determinedly they turned a blind eye to the whipping, freezing, driving snow as they got in the carriage. 'We are still high up here,' Pamela called to the driver. 'When we start to descend you will find the snow has changed to rain.'

The snow fell heavier and heavier, and the light failed quickly. The driver cursed the folly of his passengers, peering into the storm, trying to keep his horses on the road, and yet wondering which was road and which was ditch. He rounded a bend, and then the carriage gave a creak and overturned.

Shaken, Pamela and Honoria were helped out, finding themselves standing up to their knees in snow. 'There is a light over there,' Pamela shouted to one of the grooms. 'See if it is a house.'

They crouched down in the shelter of the overturned carriage. The carriage horses had been cut free and the driver stood beside them, telling them quite clearly what he thought of silly women who put the lives of men and horses at risk. The groom returned with a small bent man carrying a lantern. 'We're at the hunting box of the Duke of Ware,' he said. 'This is the lodge keeper. You ladies had better mount and make your way up to the house, and we'll follow with the baggage.'

Honoria and Pamela were thrown up into the saddles of the outriders' horses. Numb with cold, clutching the reins with their wet gloves, they urged the horses through a large gateway and through the snowdrifts of a long drive.

At last they could see the lights of a large house flickering through the snow.

Honoria slid off her mount under the welcome shelter of the portico and rang a large bell that was hanging from a rope beside the door.

'They cannot turn us away,' said Pamela, coming to join her.

The door was opened by a butler. Honoria and Pamela walked past him and into a large square hall, not wanting to stand out in the cold and argue their case. 'We are Miss Honoria Goodham and Mrs Perryworth,' said Honoria, conscious of her bedraggled clothes and her hair hanging down under her bonnet in two pleats. 'Our carriage overturned in the snow, and we are come to beg for shelter.'

'I will inform His Grace of your arrival,' said the butler, and Pamela Perryworth was conscious of the servant's eyes flicking expertly over them, debating whether to send them to the kitchen or keep them above stairs. Honoria looked back at him and raised her eyebrows haughtily.

'If you will wait in here,' said the butler, throwing open a door.

'Our coachman and outriders will be arriving shortly,' said Honoria, walking into a long saloon and making straight for the fire.

The butler bowed and left.

'It is very magnificent for a mere hunting box,' said Pamela, joining Honoria in front of the fire, stripping off her wet gloves and holding her hands out to the blaze. They looked around. There were several fine pictures, modern furniture upholstered in striped gold and white satin, marble and gilt tables, tall candelabra, and a fine French carpet in a design of pink and grey.

A footman in red and gold livery came in and placed a tray of tea and cakes on a table in front of the fire, bowed, and withdrew.

'Well, this is better,' said Honoria loudly-loudly for she was intimidated by the richness of their surroundings.

They sat down. Pamela poured tea into eggshell thin cups. She was tired and bewildered and only wanted to go to bed. She wished they were in some impersonal inn and not in a duke's home, pleading for shelter.

The butler came back in, followed by a housekeeper. 'His Grace's compliments,' he said. 'He begs you to accept the shelter of his house. The housekeeper will show you to your rooms. The maids are attending to your baggage.'

Honoria found her voice. 'And when may we have the pleasure of thanking the Duke of Ware in person?'

'I am afraid that will not be possible, miss. His Grace is indisposed. He has the fever.'

'Dear me, has the doctor been called?'

'His Grace's instructions are that he will do very well if left peacefully to recover. Now, if you are ready?'

They followed him up an oaken staircase to the bedrooms. They were, said the butler, to be given a suite of apartments on the second floor. The bedrooms, one for Honoria and one for Pamela, were divided by a sitting room and had obviously been kept ready for female guests, for they were prettily and daintily furnished, the toilet table in each bedroom being laden with bottles and lotions. Pamela dismissed the maids, saying faintly they would look after themselves, the reason being that she was all too conscious of her coarse, darned cotton underwear and did not want to expose it to the view of these ducal servants, only realizing when she went through to her own bedroom that they had already seen the rest of it, all her trunks having been unpacked and the clothes put away. She began to shiver uncontrollably and then let out a loud sneeze.

Honoria came in and looked at her with concern. Pamela's face was flushed, and her eyes were glittering. 'You must go to bed immediately,' cried Honoria. 'Oh, why did we ever drink that wine and behave so foolishly?'

Pamela weakly allowed herself to be undressed and put to bed. Honoria sat beside the bed, holding her new friend's hand until Pamela fell into an uneasy sleep.

Honoria went to her own room and brushed her hair and braided it and changed into a clean gown. She must do something good to placate this God who was so angry with her for drinking. There was one thing she could do. Her host was ill. She could see to his comfort as she had seen to the comfort of many of the sick people of the village.

She rang the bell which was promptly answered by a footman. To Honoria's request to be taken to the duke, he looked horrified and replied that his master must not be disturbed.

Cunningly, Honoria said in that case could he tell her where the duke's bedchamber was located, for she would make sure that she and her friend did not make any unnecessary noise when passing near it. The footman replied that the duke's rooms were at the end of the same corridor in which theirs was located. Honoria nodded to him in dismissal. When he had gone, she took out a book of sermons and marched out into the corridor and along to the end. In her mind's eye, she had a picture of a frail and elderly gentleman in the grip of a fever, too old and stubborn to ask for help.

* * *

The Duke of Ware, as he lay restlessly awake against his pillows, was not the kind of man, despite his wicked reputation, to think he was suffering from any sort of divine retribution.

He had caught a chill, that was all, and could only be glad his noisy guests and his mistress had departed before the snow fell. His illness, in his opinion, was nothing to do with his energetic pursuits in the hunting field or in the bedroom. He was unmarried and well aware of his reputation for romancing and hard living. He was thirty-three and thought that he might get married one day, but not yet. He was an exceptionally handsome man in a saturnine way with hair as dark as midnight, odd-colored tawny eyes, and the figure of an athlete. The fact that he had two female visitors did not interest him. His valet had reported the butler's words that a couple of provincial dowds, although no doubt ladies, had landed on his doorstep. The duke knew that the days when ladies manufactured accidents to get near him were over. His bad reputation and sarcastic tongue had seen to that. He knew himself to be a good and fair landlord. He had hardly ever been troubled by qualms of conscience and thought love was the invention of poets.

He did, however, feel miserable, with a burning forehead and an aching body.

The door opened and a figure entered and stood in the shadows of the room, surveying him.

'Who's there?' he called from the vastness of the medieval four-poster bed.

'Honoria Goodham, an it please Your Grace,' came a light, clear voice.

'Who the deuce is Honoria Goodham?'

'I am one of the ladies stranded by the storm.'

'Oh, one of the dowds. Well, my pet, I am not in the mood. Take yourself off.'

Honoria's face flamed, but she walked up to the side of the bed and looked at the duke. 'I'faith, you are a schoolgirl,' he said, looking at those long pigtails. 'What are you doing walking so boldly into a gentleman's bedchamber?'

'I am come to read to you, but first I must see to your comfort.' Honoria had been taken aback to find he was not an elderly gentleman, but a sick man was a sick man and must be cared for. She went to the toilet table and filled a basin with warm water and cologne, found a cloth, returned to the bed, and bathed the duke's forehead. He was about to protest, but her touch was gentle, and the warm water and cologne soothing. Then she ordered him to sit up and plumped up his pillows and then settled him against them. Half-amused, half-exasperated, his eyes glinted feverishly in the candlelight as he watched her take out a book of sermons. In her pleasant voice, she began to read.

She had the most beautiful eyes and ridiculously long lashes, he thought, casting an expert eye over her. He decided to humour her and listened to that soothing voice until he drifted off to sleep.

At four in the morning, he tossed and turned himself awake and felt that gentle hand bathing his forehead again. A hand held a cup to his lips and urged him to drink. He drank the posset she had ordered to be prepared for him by the surprised servants. She had laced it with a little laudanum. She continued to bathe his forehead until he fell asleep again.

During the following snowbound days, Honoria trotted cheerfully between the duke's bedroom and Pamela's, caring equally for each invalid. Concern for her patients had given her a new authority, and so the servants obeyed her commands and invalid food was presented to the duke, who was now too weak to protest. Honoria was one of those unusual people who do not need much sleep, but she managed a few hours each afternoon, lulled by the wealthy comfort of the house and the silence caused by the drifting, enveloping snow outside. Once more she was doing her duty, and her conscience was quiet. She did not see the duke as a man, only as a rather tetchy patient. That evening the snow changed to rain and the wind shifted to the southwest. She sent for the driver. He told her that it would take another couple of days at least for the roads would be impassible with floods and mud, so she tranquilly went off to wait on the duke's comfort.

The duke was rapidly recovering and no longer found this 'schoolgirl' charming. In fact, her sermons were beginning to make him restless. But courtesy bred out of a respect for her kindness stopped him from telling her so. When his servants told him the weather had turned fine and unseasonably warm and that the roads were clearing quickly, he heaved a sigh of relief.

He was up and out of bed for the first time on the day that Honoria and Pamela, also completely recovered, were due to leave.

Honoria, entering his bedchamber, was intimidated by his height, by the glory of his oriental dressing gown, by the new mocking light in his eyes, and by his brooding air of sensuality.

'As you can see, Miss Goodham,' he said, 'I no longer require your services. I gather you are taking your leave.'

'Yes, Your Grace. Mrs Perryworth and I thank you for your hospitality.'

'You are on your way to London?'

'Yes, Your Grace. We are to stay with Lady Dacey.'

'With *whom*?'

'Lady Dacey. Do you know Lady Dacey?'

His eyes glittered with a wicked light. The correct answer to that was, 'What man in London does not?' But he said aloud, 'I know her slightly. A long visit?'

'No, I am going there until the end of the Season.'

'You surely do not plan your come-out?'

'But, yes. Lady Dacey has been kind enough to say she will present me.'

He was sitting in a high-backed carved chair by the window. He made a steeple of his long white fingers and surveyed her over them. 'How old are you, child?'

'I am eighteen.'

'So old? Do you plan to read sermons to Lady Dacey?'

'If that pleases her, yes.'

He stood up and approached her. 'Good luck,' he said. 'You will need it.'

She swept him a curtsy, and he noticed that she moved with a natural grace. 'Thank you for all your hospitality,' she said, suddenly shy. 'Perhaps we shall meet again?'

'Oh, I doubt that.' He bowed and turned away and stared out of the window as if she were already forgotten.

Honoria felt quite small and grubby and depressed. She was very subdued as she climbed into the post chaise with Pamela. If London was going to be full of such grand and terrifying gentlemen, she had little hope of making a good marriage.

'I am sorry I did not meet our host,' said Pamela. 'And after all, Lady Dacey hopes you will marry a duke. But not that one! My dear, the little maid who dressed my hair told me he is considered very wicked indeed and, had we arrived a few days earlier, we would have found some rackety Corinthians and their mistresses in residence.'

Honoria tugged miserably at her pleated hair and remembered the sermon reading. She had been so anxious to be good, to clear her own conscience, that she had not paused to think what type of man she was nursing.

'I shall write to Mama this evening,' said Honoria, 'and tell her of our visit. She will be delighted.'

'Not if she knows the duke's reputation.'

'She will be in alt, I assure you. Did not Mama look fondly on the prospects of such as Mr Pomfret?'

Pamela shifted uncomfortably. 'I am here to reprove you for such remarks, but I find I cannot. It is very hard, I find, to tell right from wrong when one has been made to feel guilty about everything.' She gave a self-conscious laugh. 'Do you know, when the carriage overturned and I became ill, I thought God was punishing us.'

Honoria looked startled. 'Such a thought has been plaguing me. I wished to atone for my sins by nursing the duke. I thought our accident was divine retribution for having drunk wine.'

'I think sometimes,' said Pamela cautiously, 'that my beliefs are superstitious rather than spiritual.'

'Have we a generous amount of money for expenses on this journey?' asked Honoria.

'Yes, very generous.'

'Then when we stop for the night, I would like champagne. I have never tasted champagne.'

'Oh, Honoria!'

'We will put it to the test. We shall command the best food and the best champagne and then see what happens.'

'You are very brave.'

'Only practical. If one thinks one's fears are silly, then it is better to put them to the test. And I am going to wear my hair up. We will have a private parlour. No one will see us.'

Although they knew they were only going to see each other at dinner, both ladies worked at their appearances, Pamela curling Honoria's rippling hair and piling it on her head in one of the new classical fashions. They dressed in their finest gowns, Honoria in sprigged muslin, Pamela in grey silk, and draped shawls about their shoulders, each checking that the other had the folds of the material draped at just the right angle.

That was when the innkeeper came in, bowing and scraping and offering apologies. The chimney in the private parlour had gone on fire and the resultant fall of soot had blackened the room. There were no other private parlours available. But the company in the public dining room was very genteel, very sober. He did not cater to coach parties. It was one of England's finest posting houses. There was nothing else they could do but agree to his offer.

'This must be what it is like, going on stage,' said Honoria. 'I feel quite self-conscious.'

'You look beautiful,' said Pamela, and meant it.

Honoria appeared transformed. Her shining waves and curls shone in the lamplight, piled up on her small head, exposing her delicate white neck. Her large, deep blue eyes lent her innocent face an air of mystery.

They entered the dining room, heads held high, and were ushered to the best table in the bay of the window. Honoria relaxed once they were seated and looked cautiously around. A very ordinary sort of respectable family—father, mother, grown-up son and daughter—was at one of the tables, a grim spinster at another, what looked like a lawyer and his wife at a third, and a party of men at a fourth. Nothing to worry about.

Pamela had thought the idea of drinking champagne was only to be indulged in private and so was alarmed to hear Honoria's clear voice firmly ordering a bottle.

She glanced uneasily from behind the shelter of her fan at the men at the other table. There were four of them, all fashionably dressed, and all with that damn-your-eyes stare of the well-bred. They were looking at Honoria, with a sort of predatory expression—or rather, three of them were. The fourth was looking at

Pamela. She coloured and stared down at the table.

Honoria saw that embarrassed flush and looked across at the men. She raised her thin eyebrows haughtily and the three who had been looking at her turned away and began to talk to one another. The fourth went on looking at Pamela. He was a roguishly handsome man, not in his first youth, but almost boyish with his slender figure like an acrobat's and his head of glossy black curls. He went on looking at Pamela in an unselfconscious way, his dark eyes alight with admiration.

Honoria had another look at the vicar's wife. She had been so used to thinking of Pamela as middle-aged and colourless, despite their new-found friendship, that she saw to her surprise that Pamela was in fact looking very attractive. Her fair hair under a lace cap gleamed softly in the candlelight, and her wide brown eyes and soft mouth made her look vulnerable. Her face had lost that set, rigid look, and her mouth was no longer crimped in at the corners.

'You have a beau,' commented Honoria, 'and a very attractive one, too.'

'I wish he would not stare so,' said Pamela to the table.

'The other three stared at me,' said Honoria reflectively, 'and although I glared at them to put them in their place, I confess I rather enjoyed the novelty of being stared at. Men never looked at me so before. There is a lot to be said for having one's hair up. Here is our champagne. Drink a glass, Pamela, and forget your admirer.'

The food was excellent and the champagne tasted refreshingly innocuous. They talked about the duke's household and made up stories about his wickedness, forgetting the rest of the diners as they talked.

They finally rose to leave, and the four men promptly got to their feet as well. Heads high and cheeks flushed, Honoria and Pamela walked past them.

'We are becoming *very* sophisticated,' said Honoria happily when they had reached their bedchamber.

Pamela let out an exclamation of dismay. 'I have dropped my fan! I must have left it in the dining room. I really do not want to go back down there.'

'A servant can do that.' Honoria opened the door and called, 'Waiter!' A harrassed individual, ignoring the other peremptory cries of 'Waiter' that sounded through every English inn at all times of the day and night, rushed to attend to those the other servants were already describing as 'the pretty ladies.'

'My friend dropped her fan in the dining room,' said Honoria. 'Be so good as to retrieve it for her. It is a painted fan on ivory sticks.'

'I do hope he finds it,' said Pamela

anxiously. 'It was a present from Mr Perryworth. He will be so very angry if I lose it.'

The waiter returned after some time to say there was no sign of it. The dining room and the stairs leading to their room had been thoroughly searched.

'Oh, dear,' said Pamela. 'Do you think..?'

'If we start to think that we are being punished for drinking champagne by the loss of a mere fan, then we are run mad. Pamela! London is full of shops and shops are full of fans. I swear we can find one so like it that Mr Perryworth won't know the difference.'

'You don't know my husband,' said Pamela gloomily. 'He will know it is not the right one, and he will punish me.'

'Punish you? You are not a naughty child. How will he punish you?'

'He will refuse to speak to me for quite a long time.' Something rebellious rose up in Honoria as she looked at Pamela's sad face.

'And would that be such a bad thing, my dear? He only opens his mouth at the best of times to find fault.'

'Honoria!'

'It is true. I have said it. I don't care. I enjoyed the champagne and the stares of these men. So there. You are worrying already about what will happen to us when we return home. But it is months until the Season begins, and then it will be next summer before we need to think of heading north. I am weary of feeling bad and guilty.' She threw her arms wide. 'I am going to *enjoy* myself.'

* * *

Pamela was awakened early next morning by the bustle in the inn yard of arrivals and departures. She rose and washed and dressed and then looked out of the window. It was a clear, frosty morning.

The gentlemen of the dining room were taking their leave. The three who had looked at Honoria got into one carriage, and the one who had looked at her, said good-bye to them, while looking toward the stables as if waiting for his own carriage. One of the men on the box said something, and to Pamela's horror, the man who had stared at her took her fan out of his pocket, kissed it, flirted it in the air, and put it in his pocket again.

She swung her cloak about her shoulders and ran downstairs and out into the inn yard, just as the carriage bearing the three men bowled off and the thief of the fan was about to climb into his own, which had been brought round.

'Stop!' cried Pamela.

He swung round, his eyes beginning to dance when he saw her.

'My fan. You stole my fan.'

He executed a low bow. 'Mr Sean Delaney at your service, ma'am.'

'Thief! Give me my fan.'

He drew it from his pocket but did not hand it to her.

'What is your name, lady?'

'Mrs Perryworth.'

'Widow?'

'I am not a widow. I am a vicar's wife,' said Pamela.

'Pity. I did not exactly steal your fan, ma'am. It was a fair exchange.'

'For what, pray?'

'For stealing my heart.'

She looked up into his handsome face and merry eyes. She felt herself beginning to smile and just managed to turn it into a grimace. 'My fan,' she repeated.

He gave a shrug and passed it to her. There was a sudden break in the arrivals and departures, and they were alone in the inn yard, screened from the windows of the inn by his carriage.

He suddenly took her face firmly between his hands and kissed her soundly on the mouth, a warm, passionate kiss that burned through the hitherto unawakened vicar's wife right down to her little kid boots.

He then stood back and bowed while she stared at him in a dazed way, the fan hanging limply in one hand.

'We shall meet again,' he said, springing into his carriage and picking up the reins. 'Your driver tells me you are bound for Lady Dacey's in London. What are a vicar's wife and a young innocent doing going to stay with such as Lady Dacey?'

And without waiting for a reply, he raised his whip in salute and drove off under the arch of the inn, his head silhouetted against the glare of the frosty morning sun.

She went slowly back into the inn, wondering why she was not shocked, wondering at the gladness coursing through her.

Honoria was awake when she returned to the room. She looked at Pamela's flushed face and bright eyes and said, 'You look very well. Perhaps you should drink champagne every day.'

'I have found my fan,' said Pamela. 'One of the gentlemen, a Mr Sean Delaney, had taken it for a joke.'

'And is Mr Sean Delaney the handsome gentleman who was so fascinated by you?'

'If you mean the one who stared at me so rudely, yes.'

'I think that is so romantic.' Honoria pirrouetted about the room. 'Shall we break hearts, do you think?'

'Mr Delaney said something that was puzzling.' Pamela frowned. 'He said, "What are a vicar's wife and a young innocent doing going to stay with such as Lady Dacey?" What do you think he meant by that?'

'I do not know. But nasty Mr Pomfret made a remark about my aunt being a trollop.'

They looked at each other uneasily. Then Honoria said, 'We are worrying over nothing. Can you imagine Mama or Papa or your husband allowing us to go and stay with anyone who was other than the most respectable of ladies?'

Pamela's face cleared. 'You have the right of it. Now we can be comfortable again.'

But she did not tell Honoria about that kiss.

* * *

Two days later the Duke of Ware came back from a long day's duck shooting, wet and cold. He bathed and changed and went down to the library. He stretched his long legs out to the fire and picked up the day's post. He preferred to read his mail in the evening.

He flicked through the letters, discarding one from his mistress to read later, tossing aside invitations to events in the county, and finally cracking open one from his friend, Mr Sean Delaney, whose flamboyant seal was instantly recognizable.

After the opening salutations—the letter, the duke noticed, had been written from some inn in Bedfordshire—Mr Delaney, to the duke's amusement, began to declare his love for a vicar's wife he just met. 'Not one of your simpering misses, Charles,' he had written, 'but dainty and fragile with great eyes like pansies shining in the sweetest face you ever saw. My knight errantry is aroused, for she is to be the guest of none other than the scandalous Lady Dacey. Alas, she is still married and goes south in the role, I think, of chaperon to a young miss called Honoria Goodham, the servants at the inn having told me as much as they know. This Honoria is exceedingly beautiful, and my friends could hardly eat their dinner for goggling at her. Although this young miss was quaffing champagne, there is a purity and innocence about her that makes her a fitting companion for my beloved.

'But how are such a pair of turtledoves going to cope with Lady Dacey? She will attempt to corrupt them.'

The duke smiled cynically. Surely pursuing a married woman was enough of an attempt at corruption.

'I plan to call on them. You did say you might open up that barn of a place of yours in Grosvenor Square. Your presence would give my lady's little friend some social cachet.'

The duke read to the end and then put the letter down. Honoria Goodham had surfaced in his life again. He could not imagine his little pigtailed sermon reader drinking champagne or indeed causing three hardened rakes—he knew Delaney's friends—to stare at her in open-mouthed admiration.

It was all an intriguing puzzle. He realized that, as usual, these days, he was suffering from a dragging ennui, which he tried to exhaust by energetic days shooting or hunting.

Delaney was a rattle but never a bore. It might be amusing to see how that little puritan, Honoria Goodham, fared with such as Lady Dacey.

He decided to move to London.

CHAPTER THREE

The last stop before London had been at an inferior sort of posting house with a lumpy bed, damp sheets, and active bugs. Honoria and Pamela had spent an almost sleepless night, and by the time their carriage began to roll over the cobbles of the London streets, even the usually resilient Honoria was tired and silent.

Just in case Lady Dacey should report to her parents that she had arrived with her hair up, Honoria had once more braided it.

The carriage rolled to stop outside a tall, thin house in Hanover Square. One of the outriders hammered at the door. The ladies waited in the carriage. The door opened and a very grand footman stood there. He inclined his head as the groom talked and then called something over his shoulder. An equally magnificent footman joined him and both approached the carriage. A butler appeared on the front steps.

The groom opened the carriage door. 'Lady

Dacey is not at home, but you are to step inside. Her ladyship will see you tomorrow.'

Relief flooded both of them as if at a stay of execution. They entered the house and dimly took in the richness of their surroundings: the white and black tiled floor like a chessboard, the fire burning and the bowls of flowers, in a *hall*. Halls in Yorkshire were small, dark places, redolent of damp dog and damp coats.

Their bedchambers were warm and well-appointed. 'Everything is going to be all right,' said Honoria happily. 'I know it. No one with such a *pretty* house can be rigid or puritanical.'

The London morning dawned dark and wet and windy, with smoke swirling down into the square from the tall chimneys of the houses and a few remaining leaves, last survivors of autumn past, blowing over the cobbles.

They awoke late—for them—but were told by a French lady's maid that Lady Dacey never rose before two in the afternoon. This was all very *London* and exciting to Honoria. But she told the lady's maid that she would wear her hair braided as usual.

After a cold collation, Honoria and Pamela read all the newspapers, sitting in front of the fire in a drawing room that glittered with mirrors, gilt and marble tables, French clocks, and shiny satin upholstered furniture.

At three o'clock, both were becoming increasingly nervous. Honoria had sent their respects up to Lady's Dacey's bedchamber at two o'clock, but so far that lady had not sent any reply.

Their nervousness began to mount. They stopped reading or even pretending to read. When a footman entered, they both started in fright.

'Her ladyship's compliments,' he said. 'Her ladyship will be with you presently.'

After the footman had left, both stood up and faced the door . . . and waited, and waited.

The clocks began to chime four. Then the double doors to the drawing room were thrown open, and Lady Dacey swept in.

Honoria and Pamela stood and stared.

She was wearing a scarlet wig. She had a round pretty face, slightly marred by thick eyelids and a thin, highly painted mouth. Her eyes were pale blue with bluish whites, making them look like doll's eyes. She was dressed in dampened and transparent muslin that left very little to the imagination. Her tiny feet were shod in Roman sandals. She had a full figure and round plump arms and round plump breasts.

She stood and surveyed Honoria and Pamela, her eyebrows rising.

Both remembered their manners and curtsied low.

Lady Dacey smiled. 'Little Honoria! Why, you are a beauty! But badly in need of town bronze. Sit! Sit! Mrs Perryworth, I believe? Charmed. Now tell me about your journey.'

'We apologize for the delay in our arrival,' said Honoria, still hardly able to believe this painted and outrageous female was her mother's sister. 'Our carriage overturned in the snow, and we had to beg shelter.'

Lady Dacey yawned, a wide pink yawn like that of a sleepy cat. 'I hope you found tolerable company.'

'We were resident with the Duke of Ware.'

Lady Dacey blinked and sat up straight, those odd eyes of hers so very wide and strained with surprise that Honoria had an impulse to reach out a hand and see if she could close them, like those of a doll.

'Wicked Ware?'

'That I cannot say,' said Honoria primly. 'His Grace was ill and I had the privilege of nursing him to health.'

'Good gracious, child, the most handsome man in Britain, not to mention one of the richest, and you were on intimate terms with him.' Her eyes gleamed lasciviously. 'You were at his bedside?'

'Yes, Aunt Clarissa.'

'Do not call me that! La, I look too young to be anybody's aunt, do I not? How did you entertain Ware?'

'I read him sermons.'

'You joke!'

'Not I, Aun—I mean, my lady. They are very good sermons. The sick are in need of strengthening of the soul as well as the body.'

Lady Dacey laughed and laughed and then wiped her streaming eyes. 'You must not moralize in London, my sweeting, or you will be a laughing-stock. But to think of Ware, of all people, trapped in his sickbed, listening to sermons! Nonetheless, your news interests me greatly. Ware is not for you, of course. He needs a more mature and experienced woman of the world. Misses bore him.' She stifled a giggle. 'Particularly misses who read sermons. But I am interested in Ware . . . very. This will be an opportunity to write and thank him. Did you say you were to reside with me? Did you say I was your aunt?'

'Yes, on both counts.'

'Good to the first, bad to the second. I do not like to be known as your aunt. So aging, don't you think? Still, perhaps he will not remember. And you, Mrs Perryworth? Ah, we are to be friends. Pamela, is it not? And you will both call me Clarissa, and we will have such fun. So, Pamela, what did you think of Ware?'

'I was unfortunately ill myself, Clarissa. I had no opportunity to study our host.'

'No matter. Does he plan to come to London?'

'He said nothing to me of the matter,' said Honoria.

Lady Dacey relapsed into silence. Honoria started to speak, but Lady Dacey put her finger to her lips. After some time, she said, 'I think I might take a trip north myself. If *my* carriage were to have a mishap at Ware's gates, then he would need to entertain me.'

Pamela found her voice. 'I should point out that we were fortunate in the timing of our visit. Had we arrived a week before, then we should have found the house full of Corinthians and Cyprians, not to mention,' she blushed, 'His Grace's mistress.'

'Oh, Penelope Wilson? Her days are numbered, or so I hear. Yes, I think I shall introduce you, Pamela, to the mantua makers, the milliners, the hairdressers, and whatever you desire. They will furnish you both with fashionable clothes, and you can both work at practising your social manners while I am away.'

'But, my lady,' exclaimed Pamela, forgetting the first name request in her distress, 'neither of us know London or society or anyone. We shall be quite lost.'

'Fiddle. It is winter. What would you do were you still in Yorkshire? Read books and sew. You can do the same here. The Season is still a good way off.'

'We thank you for your generosity,' said Honoria quickly, 'and we shall do very well on our own.' She realized it would be pleasant to be shot of this outrageous aunt and get her bearings in the capital without her.

'Sensible girl. London is sadly flat at the moment. What shall we do this evening to amuse you?' She rose and went to the card rack on the mantelpiece and began to flick through the invitations with her small tapering fingers with their sharp, pointed nails.

'Ah, here we are. A musicale at Mrs Henry's. Rather dull, but you will meet a few people. Wear something simple, Honoria, and leave your hair down. Quite charming.'

Pamela guessed that Lady Dacey wanted to keep her niece looking like a schoolgirl so that her own years would seem less. She privately decided to do something about Honoria's hair and appearance while Lady Dacey was away.

The butler entered and presented a card. 'Mr Blackstock is called, my lady.'

Those china blue eyes sparkled wickedly. 'Ah, yes, I shall see him, Withers. Ladies, I am sure you would like to go for a walk or something. Withers, tell the second footman, Ben, to be ready to accompany them. Now, if you will excuse me...'

Honoria and Pamela made their exit just as a thick, coarse man, Mr Blackstock, was making his entrance.

'Goodness,' said Honoria, when they were changing into their walking dresses, 'how can Aunt bear to let any man see her in that disgraceful gown?'

'I fear such an aunt will do nothing for your social life or chances of finding a suitable husband,' said Pamela sadly.

'There is good in everyone,' replied

Honoria. 'When she returns from her visit to Ware, we must see what we can do about reforming her character.'

'Now, I would consider that a waste of time.' Pamela swung a cloak about her shoulders. 'At least the rain has stopped.'

The bustle of the London streets almost overwhelmed them. Everyone and everything moved so quickly. People on foot ran along as if pursued by bailiffs. People with carriages drove them at full tilt. The cobbled roads shook under the speed of the hackney carriages, and even a wagon went through Piccadilly at the hand-gallop.

There were few sedan chairs left plying their trade, but such as there were were still borne by aggressive Irish chairmen, running along the pavements shouting, 'Make way!' and sending passersby diving for cover.

The shops were bewildering, piled high with every luxury from every part of the world. Pamela and Honoria studied the aristocratic ladies who swept into the most expensive shops, noticing their dress and manner and wondering if they could ever pass muster in such grand company.

By the time they returned to Hanover Square, both were tired and hungry. Dinner, they learned, was at the new fashionable hour of seven. Lucille, the French lady's maid, helped them both change for the evening. Honoria envied Pamela's fashionable hairstyle and more modish appearance. She herself felt sadly provincial.

Dinner was a silent affair. Lady Dacey appeared preoccupied, although she threw several calculating looks in Honoria's direction from time to time. The journey to the musicale was only a few streets away, but Honoria was to learn that a lady never arrived on foot, no matter how short the distance. The idea of a musicale was comforting. She would not be expected to socialize much, surely, and would be allowed to sit quietly and listen to the music.

Lady Dacey was wearing a more modest gown, although the neckline was so low it showed the top half of her nipples. On entering the Henrys' house, Honoria was pleased to note that their hostess was a respectable matron, grandly but modestly gowned. She and Pamela were introduced by Lady Dacey to Mr and Mrs Henry. Mr Henry, a florid man, pinched Honoria's cheek, and Mrs Henry gave her a long, slow, assessing stare. Honoria was to become used to those stares. She could not help wondering why her outrageous aunt appeared to have social entrée to the best houses, but was to learn later that society never shut its doors on a rich countess. Someone of lesser rank would have been immediately ostracized. Having introduced them, Lady Dacey obviously considered her duties at an end. She flirted outrageously with the men and ignored the women.

They took their seats for the performance, a piano recital. The pianist, a young and romantic-looking man, raised his fingers over the keys. There was an expectant hush. He hit the first notes. Immediately the sounds of the pianoforte were lost in a great babble of gossip as each turned to his or her neighbour and began to talk. Honoria was intrigued and amused. As the music rose to a crescendo, so did the voices. At last, the musician hit the last note and immediately everyone fell silent for a few moments before applauding loudly.

'Poor man,' said Pamela. 'What is the point of getting him to play if no one listens?'

'Disgraceful,' said Honoria, quite outraged. The guests were filing through to the supper room, chattering like so many starlings on a Whitehall roof. 'We must go and thank him.'

Pamela looked uneasy. 'I do not know if it is quite the thing.'

'It is the *right* thing to do,' said Honoria firmly.

She approached the musician, who was putting away his music. Pamela followed.

Honoria held out her hand and smiled. 'I wish I could have heard what you played, sir,' she said. 'Nonetheless, I thank you for your efforts to entertain us.'

He gave her a limp handshake. He looked very tired. 'In truth, ma'am,' he said, 'I do not know why I bother to make any effort to entertain the company.'

'We will listen,' said Honoria, 'if you would like to play us something.'

He smiled suddenly and sat down and began to play a short piece by Mozart.

He had no sooner finished than Lady Dacey was upon them. 'Have you taken leave of your senses, Honoria?' she demanded. 'Leave this bandsman and join the company.'

'He is a musician, Aunt.'

'Don't call me that! Goodness, you will have people saying you are a bluestocking. Come away.'

Pamela tugged at Honoria's arm and whispered, 'People are looking. We will talk about this later.'

They joined the company in the supper room.

Pamela saw two men scrutinizing Honoria. One said to the other, 'That's a tasty piece of bait our Lady Dacey has brought with her.' She wondered what on earth they meant.

Honoria began to find the evening tedious. Everyone was relaying gossip about people of whom she had never heard, the men often talking in such broad cant they were nigh incomprehensible.

Fortunately for Honoria, the gentleman whom Lady Dacey had selected as her flirt for the evening escaped her clutches and could soon be seen talking animatedly to a young miss, and so Lady Dacey pronounced the evening sadly flat and suggested they should go home.

* * *

They arose early the next morning and spent the first part wondering when their hostess would appear and what she had planned for them. When they went down to the drawing room, the butler handed Pamela a letter.

She read it and looked at Honoria in surprise. 'Would you believe this? Lady Dacey has gone off to the north already! She has left a long list of all the people with whom she has credit, from dressmakers to stay makers, and begs us make use of them. She has also left a generous amount of money, she says, in the desk over there.'

'I should have spoken to her about the folly of trying to entrap Ware,' said Honoria sadly. 'I fear he is a bad man. At first I thought we should not rely on servants' gossip. But on reflection, I see no reason why that maid who told you about his previous visitors should lie. Furthermore, Lady Dacey accepted the existence of his mistress without a blink—in fact, even knew her name and her present standing in the duke's affections. I feel it is my duty to try to reform Aunt.'

'I do not think our hostess would think there was any reason for reform, nor would she willingly listen to any strictures from us, Honoria.'

'Nonetheless, I shall try on her return. Goodness, what are we to do on our own?'

'I shall be able to visit my sister. We will see to the ordering of our wardrobe like very grand ladies. We will send the footman to the dressmaker first and tell her to come here with designs and samples of cloth. I am sharp enough to know we do not go in person to these tradespeople; they come to us. Oh, think, Honoria. We can please ourselves in a simple way. I mean, once we have had our fittings, we can venture forth and see all the unfashionable sights such as the menagerie at the Tower, and the waxworks, and all sorts of things like that.'

Honoria gave a little shiver. She felt at that moment that her mother and father were standing in the room, looking at her with reproving eyes.

Instead, she said, 'I must write to Mama and you to Mr Perryworth. What are we to tell them of Aunt Clarissa?'

Her eyes dancing, Pamela said, 'It would be very wrong of either of us to voice any criticism of our generous hostess or to trouble either Mr Perryworth or Mr and Mrs Goodham with the intelligence that Lady Dacey is not with us. Should we write that, one or all of them might feel it their duty to come to London.'

'We couldn't have that.' Honoria brightened. 'Just think. Here we are with plenty of money, a comfortable house, carriages, and an army of servants at our disposal. And no one to criticize us or tell us what to do. Do you ever think of that cavalier who tried to steal your fan?'

'Never!' said Pamela vehemently, and then wondered why she had lied, for she thought of him often.

* * *

Over a week later, the duke was on the point of leaving for London. He was standing in the hall drawing on his gloves when a servant entered and informed him that a certain Lady Dacey was at the lodge, her carriage having broken down.

The fair Miss Goodham, he thought cynically, must have told her aunt of her visit, and so Lady Dacey, who was hardly the sort of female to be put off by his wicked reputation, had come to hunt him down.

He had no intention of meeting her. 'Give me time to get clear. Lady Dacey is at the West Lodge. I shall leave by the South. Tell her I am gone to Paris.' He turned to his butler. 'Serve Lady Dacey with refreshment and order the wheelwright to see to her carriage and send her on her way as soon as possible.'

He went outside and climbed up into the box of his travelling carriage, for he liked driving himself. The servant waited until the duke's carriage had disappeared down the other drive toward the South Lodge and then returned to

Lady Dacey, who pouted when she heard that the duke had just left for Paris.

With Napoleon incarcerated on Elba, British tourists were flocking to Paris for the first time in years. Lady Dacey thought about that, thought about the advantages of pursuing the duke to a foreign country where he might be glad to meet an attractive Englishwoman. She could not find out where the duke was staying, but high society was a small circle, and so she was confident that when she got to Paris she could easily run him to earth.

So the duke continued on his way to London. His conscience, never very active, gave a slight stab. He should really call on that impossible schoolgirl and warn her of the perils of staying with Lady Dacey and being sponsored by her for the Season. There had been harpies like Lady Dacey on the London scene in his youth. They used fresh young relatives as bait to draw men into their clutches. But he remembered the pigtails and sermon reading and shrewdly judged Lady Dacey would attempt to follow him to Paris and would probably not return before the Season. There was no immediate cause for concern about a young girl who was probably possessed of unshakeable virtue.

In fact, he would no doubt have forgotten about Honoria's existence had he not received a call from Mr Sean Delaney two weeks after he had taken up residence in London.

After asking after the duke's health and fidgeting about the room and picking up things and putting them down again, Mr Delaney finally burst out with, 'Did you receive my letter?'

'About your odd passion for some vicar's wife, yes.'

'She is in London! I have not seen her. You must help me!'

'If she is in London and resident at Lady Dacey's, then no doubt you will meet her at one of the social functions.'

'The miss she is escorting is not yet out. They do not go anywhere and La Dacey is rumoured to be in Paris. What is she doing in Paris when she has guests?'

'She thinks I am there.'

'Explain.'

'Mrs Perryworth, the love of your present life, and her charge, a Miss Honoria Goodham, arrived on my doorstep in the middle of a snowstorm, seeking shelter. I was ill with the fever at the time. I did not have the pleasure of seeing your Mrs Perryworth. However, Miss Goodham, who is a dyed-in-the-wool puritan, enlivened my sickbed by reading me sermons.'

'That pretty angel? When I saw her, she was drinking champagne and breaking hearts.'

'I find that hard to believe.'

'In any case, I dare to contemplate a rebuff. I

am here to beg you to call on them with me. It is even better than I hoped. You entertained them. It would only be polite to pay your respects.'

'Cannot you wait until the start of the Season? You will see them everywhere then.'

'That may be too late.'

'Listen, my friend, think very carefully. What is in your mind? You cannot possibly be setting out to seduce a vicar's wife. And in all charity, I feel that pair will have much to bear in the line of scandal when Lady Dacey returns.'

'You have not yet explained what Lady Dacey's visit to Paris has to do with you or why she thinks you are there.'

'She tried to emulate her niece by staging a breakdown at my gates. I had my servants inform her I had gone to Paris. If that is indeed where she is now, she is hunting me. Everyone knows she seeks another husband.'

Mr Delaney stopped his nervous pacing and swung round.

'I do not know what I am doing or what I want. I just want to see her again. One visit! One call! Is that too much to ask?'

'Very well.' The duke capitulated. 'One call. Any folly that happens afterward is entirely your affair.'

* * *

'I do not know if I like it. Mama will be furious,' said Honoria, looking nervously in the mirror.

Despite reminders to Pamela that Lady Dacey expected Honoria to wear her hair down, Pamela had summoned one of London's leading hairdressers to give Honoria a fashionable crop. Her hair was a cap of soft curls, framing her face.

'You will become used to it,' said Pamela. 'You look like a young lady now. No one could ever mistake you for a schoolgirl.'

'I feel it is all *wrong*,' complained Honoria. 'We have spent a fortune on gowns, hats, pelisses, shoes and gloves.'

'We have not yet spent enough,' said Pamela firmly. She had become very worldly-wise after dealing with tradesmen and scrutinizing fashion magazines. A good eye for dress, hitherto held in check because the vicar preferred to see her attired only in sober clothes, had served Pamela well. She now ran Lady Dacey's mansion with the same competent ease that she ran the vicarage. Lady Dacey's servants, who had never known before such firm but considerate authority, obeyed all her orders cheerfully and privately hoped their mistress would stay in Paris for as long as possible.

Honoria was wearing a new cambric frock of the same blue as her eyes and over it a Spanish vest of blue velvet, as that new fashion in short jackets was called. She stood up and crossed to the window and looked down into the square, 'The time for calls,' she said. 'At least we do not have to cope with that. We know no one, and nobody knows us.'

'Except my sister,' said Pamela, and then fell silent, thinking of how her sister had changed so much. Amy had become a fashionable invalid, lying in a darkened room, surrounded by bottles of medicines. She could not help remembering what friends they had been in their youth and how merry Amy used to be. And one could not blame Amy's husband for the change. He was all that was kindness and concern. In order to think of something less distressing, she remembered an item of news. 'I see from the social column that Ware is in Town,' said Pamela.

Honoria turned away from the window, her eyes widening. Then she laughed. 'I wonder if he came to London to escape my aunt. But if he is here, she must surely be expected back soon.'

Pamela stifled a sigh. 'I hope we are all going to get on well together. Drop all ideas of reform, Honoria. You will only irritate her and she will think you sadly provincial. Perhaps some people do not have a conscience to reach.'

'That is not true,' said Honoria stubbornly. 'There is good in everyone.'

'Does not Clarissa *frighten* you?'

'My aunt? Good gracious, no.'

'I think she should. Forgive me for speaking so harshly about your relative, who has been very generous, but I think she is selfish and decadent, and I distrust her motive in inviting you here.'

'Fustian. Motive? What motive can she have other than a sort of careless generosity? Yes, I admit she dresses in a scandalous manner, but no one else at that musicale seemed to find anything out of the way.'

'A title and money will open all doors,' said Pamela with newfound London cynicism.

Honoria laughed. 'It is the very *foreignness* of the capital that is giving you fancies. Aunt Clarissa lives on her own now and has possibly no female friend to advise her. This is not like our dear Yorkshire.'

'No, it is not. We have money and freedom for the first time in our lives,' Pamela tartly pointed out. 'But I warn you: Clarissa could prove to be a dangerous woman.'

'I assure you, you will find that under all that paint is a certain amount of goodness,' said Honoria firmly.

A servant scratched at the door and entered. 'If you please, ladies,' he said, 'His Grace, the Duke of Ware, and a Mr Delaney have called.'

They looked at each other wide-eyed. Then Honoria said, 'Tell them we shall be with them presently. Put them in the Green Saloon.'

CHAPTER FOUR

'You can feel the wicked lady is not in residence,' murmured the duke, looking around the Green Saloon, which Honoria and Pamela had begun to favor over the drawing room.

Bowls of hothouse flowers scented the air. There was a selection of magazines and books on a table, embroidery on a tambour frame by the window, and music spread open on the piano.

The duke then began to feel a mixture of amusement and slight consternation as Mr Delaney fussed and fidgeted, jumping up to the mirror to adjust his cravat, sitting down, only to jump up again and tease his curls with a comb.

He had seen his friend in the throes of love, or what appeared to be love, for some fashionable beauty, but had never seen him so reduced to the state of a nervous schoolboy.

The door opened, and the ladies entered. The duke rose to his feet, staring at Honoria as if he could not believe his eyes. The schoolgirl had become a woman and a beautiful one at that. Her face was framed by an aureole of soft curls, and her deep blue eyes were fringed with those long dark lashes, making her look more sensual than innocent. The little Spanish jacket hinted at an excellent bosom, a more seductive way of dressing than any of Lady Dacey's low necklines. She also looked at him as no other woman had ever looked at him since he had come into the dukedom, with open, welcoming friendliness, without flirtation or guile.

With reluctance, he turned to Pamela, who was curtsying to him. He found her very pretty and appealing but could see nothing in her to explain his friend's obsession. The usually gallant ladykiller who was Mr Delaney was blushing like a girl with delight and saying over and over again that it was wonderful to see her.

But Honoria was not so calm as she appeared. The duke's sinister good looks struck her somewhere in the region of her midriff. Before, she had not looked on him as a man, only as a patient. Now she was aware of the strength of his figure and face and of the attractive brooding quality of his gaze.

Pamela asked the gentlemen to be seated. 'Where is Lady Dacey?' asked the duke. He had no intention of telling them that *he* knew, but wondered if they had been part of the plot.

Pamela looked uneasy but Honoria said quickly, 'Lady Dacey has gone to visit a friend in the north.'

'She's in Paris,' said Mr Delaney, looking around in surprise and catching a warning look from the duke.

'Paris! What is she doing in *Paris*?' exclaimed Honoria.

'Quite a number of English have gone to Paris,' said the duke smoothly. 'It is very fashionable. But how do you go on, Miss Goodham, with no one to sponsor you? Mr Delaney, who is a reliable authority, assures me you are to be seen nowhere.'

'We have been kept busy arranging our wardrobes and sightseeing. We are most unfashionable,' said Honoria. 'There will be time enough for fashion later.'

'Still,' said the duke, 'Lady Dacey should be here nursing the ground for you, introducing you to London's hostesses.'

'I am sure we shall manage,' said Pamela quickly, avoiding Mr Delaney's burning gaze.

The duke felt a sudden pang of sympathy for these correct ladies who had only each other for company. He surprised himself by saying, 'You should go out. I am sure Mr Delaney and I would be delighted to escort you to Drury Lane. Grimaldi is appearing in the pantomime *Mother Goose*. We need not attend the play, if you wish—just the pantomime, as an introduction to London life.' The pantomime was always put on after the play.

Mr Delaney was about to object to such unsophisticated entertainment but at the light in Pamela's eyes, he fell silent.

'A pantomime,' breathed Pamela. 'I have never seen a real one, only Richardson's wagons at fair time.' She half closed her eyes, remembering one of the rare excitements of her youth when John Richardson's wagons came rumbling into the village. Clutching one of the housemaid's hands, she had stood under a Gothic arch of lamps outside the tent while the maid paid over two ninepences to a stout gentleman. Then the maid indulgently gave the young Pamela the two cardboard cheques so that she would have the honour of delivering them into the hands of none other than Harlequin himself, glittering with spangles and dazzling with many colours. But this was nothing to the glories of the inside amid the smell of sawdust and orange peel, where the first play being over, the lovers united, the ghost appeased, the baron killed, and everything happy ever after—the pantomime itself began! She half smiled remembering the opening scene of deep gloom where a crafty magician holding a young lady in bondage was revealed, studying an enchanted book to the sound of a gong. Then what a thrill as the magician transformed the monster into a clown. It did not matter that the stage was three yards wide and four deep, Pamela never saw it; only the fantasy, wrapped up in the joy of laughing at that delicious clown.

And Grimaldi at Drury Lane was the king of clowns!

'I do not think...' began Honoria cautiously, but Pamela said urgently, 'I am sure it would be quite correct for us to go, Honoria. It is *comme il faut*, is it not, gentlemen? I do not wish to lead Honoria into doing anything unconventional. She is not yet out.'

'She has your excellent presence as chaperon, Mrs Perryworth,' said the duke. 'The piece lasts only ninety minutes. We will convey you there and back. The play that precedes it is not very popular. There will not be many fashionables there, but even if there are, there can be nothing to occasion comment.'

'In that case, we will go,' said Pamela, her eyes shining.

'Thank you, Your Grace,' said Honoria dutifully, but she felt another burden had been added to her conscience. Pamela was a married lady and had no right to look so elated and happy.

The duke rose to take his leave. Mr Delaney got to his feet as well. They bowed. The ladies curtsied, and then they left.

'Now, Pamela,' said Honoria severely, 'I do not think it all the thing for you to be escorted by Mr Delaney. He is in love with you, and he must not be.'

'Mr Delaney is the type of gentleman who has to fancy himself in love,' said Pamela, although she blushed guiltily. 'Oh, Honoria, humour me! At the end of our stay in London, I must return and take up my old life. With any luck, you will be engaged to be married and can look forward to happiness. I am only borrowing happiness. I am not going to have an affair or anything scandalous like that. I am much too respectable and timid. Besides, to be seen out with a duke—that is, if anyone who matters sees us—it will establish our social credentials in a way that I am sure Lady Dacey cannot.'

'Come now,' admonished Honoria. 'Remember the duke's reputation.'

'A rake is never considered scandalous,' said Pamela. 'You will be safe in his company, my dear. You are guarded by me. I am sure a man of his years and reputation is not interested in a young miss who has not yet made her come-out.'

And Honoria, who really wanted to go to the pantomime, was glad to have her fears put to rest, or rather, to pretend to herself that they had been.

* * *

It was exciting to prepare for the evening, to put on new theatre gowns. Honoria wore a gown of lilac jaconet with a low neckline and six deep flounces at the hem, and Pamela was dressed in blue muslin embroidered at the neck and hem with seed pearls. Pamela wore one of the new Turkish turbans on her head and Honoria a Juliet cap made of gold wire and pearls. Lady Dacey's maid had gone with her to Paris, but Pamela sent for the hairdresser to arrange their hair for the evening.

As they waited nervously in the Green Saloon, each with a magnificent cashmere shawl draped around her shoulders, Pamela tried to remain calm. She was not doing anything wrong, she told herself repeatedly, although the stern and reproving face of her husband was always before her mind's eye.

Honoria, aware of her friend's heightened colour and shining eyes, felt the elder of the two. With a wisdom beyond her years, she dreaded the effect of the attractive Mr Delaney on such a lady as Pamela, who had never had any fun or laughter in her life. Honoria remembered the chill air of the vicarage and the way the vicar crept softly about, always seeking fault. Her preoccupation made her treat the duke rather coolly, and at first he was piqued and then amused at himself for being so put out by the seeming indifference of a chit of a girl.

Contrary to the duke's expectation, there were a great number of fashionables there as they took their seats in a box. People openly stared. Honoria had forgotten about that social stare. Some raised lorgnettes and one man even trained a telescope on their box.

But then the pantomime started and Honoria forgot about everything else. In later years, she was to try to tell her children about the magic of Grimaldi without success. It was not what he *said* that was so funny: it was what he *was*. There he stood, looking out at the candlelit audience, with 'a thousand odd twitches and unaccountable absurdities oozing at every pore' of his clownish mask. Above his rolling eyes were two ridiculous eyebrows that would 'go up and down like a pair of umbrellas or one would ascend, and the other remain to superintend a wink.'

His voice was another weapon. Future biographers would describe it, variously, as 'husky with constant laughing'; 'richly thick and chuckling like the utterance of a boy laughing, talking and eating custard at once'; or 'a gin voice, heaved from the very bottom of his chest.'

So with all his heady exuberance of animal spirits and the kind of laugh that made the whole house laugh with him, Grimaldi kept one eye on fantasy and one on reality: he never allowed the audience to forget for long that he *knew* it was all a game and that they were playing it, too.

And Honoria and Pamela laughed the grim years away, laughed until they held their sides, laughed until they cried. The duke was at first amused at their innocent enjoyment, for he considered himself too old and sophisticated to be captured by such childish folly, but soon he found himself laughing helplessly.

By the time the transformation scene arrived with all the cast descending a staircase on the stage to take their bows, the duke and Mr

Delaney had recovered, but their more unsophisticated guests leaned forward, drinking in the glory of the spangled costumes.

When the deafening applause had died down at last, Pamela turned to Mr Delaney and said simply, 'Thank you.'

He raised her hand to his lips and kissed it. Pamela finally shyly withdrew her hand, but her eyes were warm and glowing.

'Yes, indeed, thank you,' said Honoria briskly, anxious to get Pamela away. 'A most enjoyable evening.'

Pamela, afraid of her emotions, was silent on the road home and Honoria, worried about Pamela, was silent also. She rallied enough when they reached Hanover Square to thank both the duke and Mr Delaney again.

'We must find something else to entertain you,' said the duke. He had only meant it as a piece of empty gallantry, but to his surprise Honoria said, 'I am afraid that will not be possible. We have much to do. Come, Pamela.'

And like a stern matron, Honoria urged Pamela before her and into the house. The door shut behind them with a firm bang.

The duke was amazed. Never had any girl or woman turned down the chance of seeing him again.

'We cannot leave it like that,' exclaimed Mr Delaney.

'Oh, but I think we must.' The duke propelled him gently to the waiting carriage.

'As Miss Goodham firmly pointed out, they will be too busy. And that, my friend, is your fault. You cannot go around courting vicars' wives.'

'I will not be so obvious again.' Mr Delaney struck his heart, to the amusement of two tall footmen passing by. 'I shall be devious and circumspect and hide my passion!'

'Do that. But do not involve me in the plot. Despite my wicked reputation, I have never seduced a respectable female in my life.'

No sooner were the words out of his mouth than he wondered what it *would* be like to make love to someone as pure and innocent as Honoria.

He assured himself it would be a bore, got Mr Delaney into the carriage, and drove off.

* * *

Alas, for Mr Delaney, Pamela's recently dormant conscience came back in full strength. She refused to see him and would only go out in the carriage with Honoria after the servants had been out to check that he was not lurking anywhere in the square.

But London, although thin of company, was already beginning to buzz about the wicked duke and the unknown innocent. The duke's reputation might shock in the country, but in the heady atmosphere of London, ambitious mamas were prepared to forget it to secure a title and a fortune for their daughters. Eyebrows were raised when the spies finally reported that the young lady was a Miss Honoria Goodham, her chaperon was a Mrs Perryworth, and that Miss Goodham was the niece of the outrageous Lady Dacey. Speculation was rife. To get close to the duke was surely possible by befriending these ladies. Mr Delaney, questioned about the pair, was singularly uncommunicative, not wanting to talk about his love and casually dismissing Honoria as 'some chit of an heiress.'

Now the mothers of marriageable sons came alive. An heiress! Miss Goodham did not go anywhere socially, but maids reported to mistresses that the best of dressmakers, mantua makers, milliners, and hairdressers had been flocking to the mansion in Hanover Square. Honoria's status as heiress was therefore confirmed.

A few cards began to arrive, and then more and then more.

'We should accept,' said Pamela as they went through them.

Honoria primmed her lips in disapproval. 'If we start to go about in society, you will no doubt encounter Mr Delaney, and that will not do.'

Pamela felt a sudden wave of fury. Honoria had gone on like a stern guardian since the outing to the pantomime. She had read sermons aloud. In fact, the book of sermons was lying open on the table beside her, no doubt in preparation for another moral reading.

'If we do not go about,' Pamela said severely, 'then the Season will be upon us. If you return unwed, then no doubt your parents will offer you again to Mr Pomfret, a fate I am beginning to think you thoroughly deserve.'

'Pamela!'

'It is *my* life,' said Pamela, striking her breast. 'Mine! I am weary of being lectured to and moralized over. Here!' She stood up, picked up the book of sermons, ran to the window, opened it, and threw the book out into the square.

'There!' she said, swinging round, her face flushed. 'I am now going to Hatchard's in Piccadilly and I am going to buy one of the latest novels, so there! I have never been allowed to read fiction, and I am going to start now.'

When Pamela had swept out of the room, Honoria sat down heavily, nursing a feeling of dread, which she persuaded herself was fear for Pamela's welfare rather than any trepidation at the thought of meeting the wicked duke again.

It was Pamela who selected their first invitation, to a ball at Lord and Lady Buchan's. Lady Buchan, a correct Scottish matron, had called to pay her respects. There was nothing about her to alarm Honoria, who did not take into consideration that Lady

Buchan had two unwed sons in their early twenties.

'I sometimes fear we have been over-extravagant,' ventured Honoria, looking at their new gowns.

'Nonsense,' said Pamela with her newfound tetchiness. 'This is our first public appearance—the pantomime does not count—and we must make the best of it. Only see the number of invitations we have! What on earth can your aunt be thinking of to remain so long in Paris! Well, I am determined to ingratiate myself with as many notables as possible this evening, for I fear it is beginning to look as if I shall have to bring you out myself.'

Honoria, as a debutante, was obliged to wear white and envied Pamela her rustling lilac silk gown, but Pamela thought Honoria looked enchanting in a simple Grecian robe of white muslin embroidered with a gold key pattern and worn over a white silk slip. She had little gold slippers on her feet and a headdress of gold leaves on her hair, that soft brown hair that now framed her face in delicate curls.

Pamela sighed when she saw her, her anger and bad temper fading away. 'You will break hearts,' she said. 'Lady Dacey has the right of it. You could marry a duke.' Immediately the words were out, she regretted them, for a shadow clouded Honoria's eyes and Pamela thought she was thinking of Mr Delaney when, in fact, Honoria had been reminded of the

Duke of Ware.

Both were, however, looking forward to the ball without much trepidation, for Lady Buchan had seemed such a comfortable, sensible lady and she had promised 'not a very large affair. A few couples.'

Their nervousness did not begin until the carriage set them down in the courtyard of an enormous mansion in Piccadilly, hard by the Marquis of Queensberry's and overlooking Green Park. Flambeaux blazed from sconces on the walls and the great house was lit from top to bottom. Dance music sounded out into the night. The very air seemed to crackle with that particular sort of excitement London held in the evening, an excitement generated by several thousand people, rich and poor alike, determined to make merry. In an age when death lurked around every corner, all took their pleasures as enthusiastically as they could.

They went into a vast hall and were ushered to a side room to leave their cloaks. One of Lady Dacey's maids, who had accompanied them, helped them to make last-minute touches to their hair.

'It's like preparing to go on stage,' said Honoria with a nervous giggle. 'Or so I imagine an actress must feel. I thought this was supposed to be a quiet affair.'

'Goodness,' remarked Pamela as they emerged back into the hall and looked up the long winding stair to the ballroom, 'if this is a quiet affair, what is a *grand* London ball going to be like?'

'Oh, my stars!' cried Mr Delaney, a few moments later. 'They are arrived!'

The duke raised his quizzing glass. There was a luminosity about Honoria, he thought. She made every other woman in the room look shop-soiled, over-painted, fussy. Rose petal skin, huge blue eyes, and oh, that mouth, soft and delicate and pink and untouched. Faith, he reflected wryly, I am become a lecherous old man.

'Do ask Miss Goodham for a dance,' urged Mr Delaney. 'It would establish her social credentials.'

'I doubt if Miss Goodham needs my help,' said the duke, aware of the heightened interest of nearly every man in the ballroom. 'Oh, very well. Don't tug at my sleeve in that irritating way.'

He walked across the ballroom. Both ladies sank into low curtsies. The duke bowed. 'Miss Goodham, may I humbly beg the favour of this dance?'

A smile rose to Honoria's lips, only to disappear as the quadrille was announced. The quadrille was a new dance, and she had not yet learned the steps. Conscious of all eyes on them, she stammered out, 'I must refuse, Your Grace.'

With a look of frozen hauteur, he made

another bow and stalked off. A chattering rose and fell about Pamela and Honoria.

'Now you cannot dance at all!' exclaimed Pamela.

'But just *this* dance,' protested Honoria. 'Why did we not engage a dancing master to teach us the steps of the quadrille?'

'It does not matter,' said Pamela gloomily. 'You have refused a gentleman a dance. That means you cannot dance with anyone else.'

'Why did you not tell me this!'

'I thought you knew. If only you had told Ware you did not know the steps—then all would have been forgiven. We had best go and sit by the wall. The evening will not be wasted, for we can study how the other ladies go on.'

'Impertinent little minx,' the duke was saying to Mr Delaney.

'I cannot understand it.' Mr Delaney shook his head.

'You had best not ask Mrs Perryworth to dance or you will meet with the same rebuff.'

'Perhaps Miss Goodham and Mrs Perryworth do not know the steps of the quadrille. It has not yet been introduced at Almack's.'

'Fustian. The waltz was around for years before it was introduced at Almack's. It is a wonder they do not still perform only minuets there.'

'I shall try my luck at the next dance.'

The quadrille lasted half an hour, giving

Honoria and Pamela ample time to observe the elegance of the dancers and the intricacy of the steps.

Pamela was conscious of Mr Delaney with every fibre of her being. She tried to conjure up a picture of her husband and, unfortunately for her, succeeded in doing so to such effect, that all it did was give Mr Delaney added charm.

The Duke of Ware, thought Pamela, was not for Honoria. He was too old—in his thirties—and had a bad reputation. Honoria needed someone as young and innocent as herself. But what young gentleman, she wondered uneasily, on this frivolous London scene was going to fall in love with a young lady whose idea of entertainment was reading sermons? She had to admit that the duke was looking very handsome in his black evening dress of coat, silk breeches, and white stockings with gold clocks.

At last the quadrille was over. The dancers promenaded around the room. Then a country dance was announced.

Mr Delaney approached them and bowed. 'May I beg you for this dance, Mrs Perryworth?' Pamela felt her duty was at Honoria's side. But she could hardly add insult to injury by refusing the duke's friend.

She smiled and rose and took his arm, and Honoria was left alone on her little gilt chair. She was conscious of many stares in her direction, of whispers, of the fact that the row of dowagers across from her were leaning forward from time to time to scrutinize her. A lump rose in her throat, and she felt young and defenceless.

Pamela was separated from Mr Delaney by the figures of the dance, but when they were promenading round the room after it was over, as was the custom, she said hurriedly, 'Miss Goodham is overset. She did not mean to be rude. This is her first London ball, and she—neither of us has learned the steps of the quadrille. Please explain to the duke what the problem was. I fear he is angry with her.'

'Of course he is. But I will see what I can do.'

But when Mr Delaney went in search of the duke, he found that gentleman was already leading a young miss onto the floor. Pamela went back to sit with Honoria but discovered to her confusion that she was immediately approached by a guards officer who asked her to dance.

'Please go,' whispered Honoria. 'I shall do very well.' But she felt miserable as Pamela was led off. She felt almost naked, sitting alone. She longed to dance, to mingle with the other dancers, to be part of the ball. She had plenty of opportunity to observe how well the duke danced, how his partner sparkled up at him, how intrigued he seemed to be with her.

That dance finished. Mr Delaney waited his moment and then approached the duke. 'Miss Goodham does not know the steps of the quadrille,' he said urgently. 'She is too naive, too gauche, to know how to say so. Now she is in social disgrace—and at her first ball! She will need all the help she can get, particularly if that harridan, Lady Dacey, returns in time to sponsor her. Pray explain to Lady Buchan what is amiss and then ask Miss Goodham for another dance.'

'And risk being cut a second time by some provincial, sermonizing chit? No, I thank you.'

'Just this once. For me. It would mean so little to you and so much to her. Do this for me. You need never talk to her again afterward.'

'Oh, very well.' The duke sighed and went in search of his hostess. Lady Buchan listened to him with relief. She had urged her sons to dance with the new heiress and then found they could not as Miss Goodham had refused the duke. But if all were put right . . .

'Such an easy mistake for a young miss to make,' said Lady Buchan indulgently, 'and so good of you to explain matters. Let us go and talk to Miss Goodham.'

'It is a waltz,' said the duke sourly. 'Do you think she knows the steps to that?'

'Oh, I am sure she does, and she has my permission to dance it.'

Pamela saw the duke and Lady Buchan approaching before Honoria did and her heart quailed, dreading a lecture. She could feel all eyes on them.

Honoria looked up to see the duke standing

over her. 'His Grace informs me you do not know the steps to the quadrille,' said Lady Buchan, 'but he hopes you know the steps to the waltz.'

'Yes, yes I do,' said Honoria, looking flustered.

'Then will you favour me with this next dance, Miss Goodham?'

The duke held out his hand.

She rose with one graceful fluid movement and took his hand. He put one arm at her waist and smiled down into her eyes. Honoria had only danced the waltz before at country assemblies. Her first steps faltered until that grip at her waist tightened. She felt suddenly light-hearted. There was nothing to fear. She felt oddly safe, held in his arms, safe from prying eyes and avid gossip.

Pamela for once was hardly aware of Mr Delaney as she circled the floor with him, so anxiously did she watch Honoria. 'Look at me,' commanded Mr Delaney. His dark grey eyes sparkled as they looked down into hers. She involuntarily clutched his hand hard, feeling almost as if she were drowning. This will never do, she thought breathlessly, quickly lowering her eyes.

Honoria felt a little tug of loss inside her when the dance finished and reality came rushing back. 'You dance beautifully,' he said, as he led her round the room. 'But you must hire a dancing master and learn the steps of the quadrille. Is there no word from Lady Dacey?'

'None whatsoever,' said Honoria. She glanced up at him shyly. 'I thank you for being so forgiving. It appears that Mrs Perryworth and I will likely have to cope with the London Season on our own. I should not have liked to start my social life in disgrace.'

Did she know how alluring she was, he wondered, with those huge trusting eyes? Probably not. She had an unconscious sensuality of movement that, combined with her unawakened air, made his senses quicken in a way that disturbed him. He felt his years. He thought briefly of his mistress and felt unworthy of this innocent creature, and then angry with himself for entertaining such uncomfortable thoughts. He saw Lord Herne approaching and frowned. Herne was a rich lecher. He asked Honoria to dance, and she accepted prettily. The duke saw the way Herne's eyes slid slowly over Honoria's body as he led her away and felt like calling him out.

That one dance with Honoria he had planned to be the last he ever had with her. But he told himself she should be warned against such as Herne and that Mrs Perryworth appeared too unworldly to cope with London's dangerous men.

He knew that he was occasioning comment by asking Honoria to dance again so soon, but he did not care. It was a lively country dance that she performed with ease, crossing hands with him and dancing down the middle of the set, that flimsy gown of hers flying out around her supple body. He contented himself until the promenade and then began, 'Miss Goodham, as you and Mrs Perryworth are new to Town, I feel I should warn you against such gentlemen as Lord Herne. He has a bad reputation.'

'It is all very puzzling,' sighed Honoria. 'He seemed very kind. But you, Your Grace, have a wicked reputation and yet you also seem kind.'

'I beg your pardon!'

'I believe,' went on Honoria blithely, 'that the week before we arrived, you had a house party consisting of Cyprians, your mistress, and various Corinthians. So fortunate we did not arrive stranded on your doorstep at the same time, was it not?'

'You are behaving badly,' he said harshly.

She looked at him, wide-eyed. 'But . . . but it is a logical observation.' She looked across at Lord Herne. He was a tall, spare man with a thin mouth and cold eyes. 'Lord Herne did not say anything he ought not,' she gave a nervous laugh to try to lighten the atmosphere. 'Perhaps the most wicked gentlemen are socially the kindest.'

'Miss Goodham, I hope this is the very last time I have to tell you this. No young lady ever refers to a man's mistress, is that understood?'

'I am sorry.' She hung her head. 'I have so much to learn.'

The duke saw Archie Buchan approaching,

one of Lady Buchan's sons, tall, young, fresh-faced, and only two years older than Honoria, or so he guessed. He found himself saying quickly, 'I would be of further service to you, Miss Goodham. Will you come driving with me tomorrow?'

'I should like that above all things,' said Honoria politely.

Honoria found Archie Buchan a relief. He was a cheerful young man with a mop of blond curls. He looked at her with open admiration and danced rather badly, which gave her a pleasant feeling of superiority. At the end of the dance, he asked her to go driving with him on the following day, and she felt genuinely sorry that she had to refuse.

She was never without a partner for the rest of her stay at the ball. She and Pamela left at two in the morning, surprised to see that they were among the first to leave. 'Now I understand why everyone sleeps until two in the afternoon,' yawned Pamela in the carriage home. 'You were such a success, Honoria. I was proud of you. There is only one thing that gives me a certain disquiet. I overheard you being described as "the new heiress." Now, I know you have probably a good dowry by country standards, but I doubt if it would be considered very great in this profligate society. Did you note Lady Buchan's gown? The clasps on her overdress were of real gold and diamonds.'

'Just tittle-tattle,' said Honoria. 'They will soon forget it. I had such fun. I did so want to go driving with Mr Buchan—Mr Archie Buchan, that is—tomorrow.'

'And why couldn't you?'

'I promised to go driving with Ware.'

'Oh, my dear, is that wise? There is no hope there, you know.'

Honoria laughed. 'Pooh, just think how it will add to my social consequence to be seen driving with a duke!'

CHAPTER FIVE

Pamela received the Duke of Ware the following afternoon. She wondered uneasily whether she ought to ask him his intentions or not, whether she should even allow Honoria to go driving with such a man. But a duke was a duke, and to snub such a one would not help Honoria's social position, and besides, what could happen during a drive in the park? The day was fine and unseasonably warm.

Honoria, wearing a carriage gown of golden brown velvet with a small Elizabethan ruff at the neck, entered the room. The duke stood up and bowed. He seemed detached, formal, almost as if he were already regretting his invitation, and Pamela felt herself relax.

She stood at the window and watched them

drive off in the sunshine. Honoria unfurled a parasol, screening her face. With a little sigh, Pamela turned away from the window, feeling lonely, feeling the very *foreignness* of London, half wishing herself home in Yorkshire and back in her familiar shackles. A letter from her husband lay on the table, still unread.

She picked it up reluctantly, just as the butler announced Mr Sean Delaney. She coloured up guiltily, feeling the letter suddenly heavy in her hand. She could not very well refuse to see the duke's friend when that friend had been instrumental in saving Honoria from social disgrace. Mr Delaney came in. 'Faith, you look a picture,' he said, seizing her hands and kissing them.

Pamela drew back. 'Mr Delaney, I must make one thing very clear. I am a married lady, and your attentions are over-warm.'

'I forgot myself,' he said cheerfully. He took a turn about the room in his restless way and then swung round again to face her. 'I have it!' he cried. 'We'll strike a bargain.' He held out a hand. 'We will be friends. Come! I can be useful to you and Miss Goodham. A platonic friend to escort you about until the Season is over.'

His expression seemed so open and so honest. She found her lips curving in a smile. A still small voice in her brain was warning her that she was seizing on his offer of friendship as a way of keeping him close, but the rest of her mind stubbornly rejected that idea. She and

Honoria were in need of introductions and guidance through this London maze. 'I accept your terms,' she said gaily.

'In that case, go and put on your bonnet. It is a fine day, and Ware and Miss Goodham should not be the only ones to enjoy the sunshine.'

* * *

Honoria, innocent as she was, could not help noticing the interest her arrival in the park was causing among the fashionables and was human enough to enjoy it. The duke drove very well, pointing out various notables to her. The sun shone down on jewels and carriages and some of the finest horseflesh in the world.

For the first time since she had come to London, Honoria felt free of her chilly upbringing, of the fear of Mr Pomfret. Only a little shadow in her mind told her that somehow she must marry before the Season was over, but the Season at least had not even begun. She thought instead of Archie Buchan. He had called to pay his respects earlier, his eyes glowing with admiration. He had come to press his mother's invitation to a turtle dinner, and both Pamela and Honoria had accepted with delight. What a contrast young Mr Buchan was to Mr Pomfret, thought Honoria. So affectionate, so gay, so *young*.

'You are looking unfashionably happy,'

came the duke's amused voice. 'Do not you know you are supposed to assume a world-weary air?'

'I am enjoying myself,' said Honoria simply. 'Home seems so very far away.'

'And that makes you happy?'

'I honour my parents, Your Grace, but in truth, they nearly arranged a most unhappy marriage for me. Had not Lady Dacey been kind enough to invite me, then I should already be married to a man I despise.'

'I do not want to dim your happiness, but that may yet happen.'

'How so? Lady Dacey cannot constrain me to marry anyone.'

'You do not yet know the pressures that can be brought to bear on a young miss before the end of the Season. You will be expected to repay your hostess's efforts on your behalf by marrying well, and "well" does not necessarily mean the man of your choice.'

Honoria glanced up at him from under her long eyelashes. 'Would you say the Honourable Archie Buchan is a good prospect?'

He felt a stab of irritation. She was treating him like some elderly uncle. 'He is a pleasant young man, but it is well known the Buchans want heiresses for their sons.'

'Oh,' said Honoria in a small voice. Then she brightened. 'I am not exactly an heiress, but . . .' She bit her lip. She could hardly start to discuss the size of her dowry. 'In any case, Mr Buchan called today to invite us to a turtle dinner on Saturday. He came with a most pressing invitation from Lady Buchan. Would ... would an heiress need to have a *great* deal of money?'

'Lord Chemford lost twenty-five thousand pounds at White's the other night. Those are the sort of figures you have to think of in this society.'

Honoria lowered her parasol slightly to shield her expression. Her dowry was fifteen hundred pounds, a healthy sum in the wilds of Yorkshire. But she refused to be depressed. So she was not an heiress. She had never pretended to be, and Lady Buchan was kind and her son, delightful and warm-hearted. Her good humour restored, she dipped her parasol and said, 'And you, Your Grace. What of you? Do you plan to marry at last?'

'I do not know,' he said curtly, but aware that a short time ago he would have replied, 'Of course not.' Although he had complained about her sermons, it had been pleasant to be nursed, to have a lady running his household, instead of housing some resident Cyprian, despised by his servants. Honoria was too young—he had no taste for young misses—but for the first time he was beginning to entertain the idea that a woman of his own rank and birth might be a good idea. The dukedom needed an heir.

And yet this young chit's very indifference to him was galling. He decided to flirt. 'You are looking very beautiful today, Miss Goodham,' he said. 'I am the envy of all men.'

'And the despair of some ladies,' remarked Honoria. 'Who is that lady in the blue gown who is scowling at me?'

He looked across the park, following her gaze. There was his mistress, Penelope Wilson, driving a smart little carriage drawn by a white horse. He gave her a nod as they bowled past. He had not been to see her since his arrival in London.

'A Miss Wilson,' he said.

'Oh, *Penelope* Wilson—your mistress.'

'Miss Goodham, I am not charmed by gaucherie.'

'Nor by innocence, it would appear,' retorted Honoria, thinking of Miss Wilson's disgracefully low-cut gown and painted face.

'You displease me,' he said frostily.

'Then please take me home,' replied Honoria equably, and in that moment he could have slapped her.

He drove smartly out through the gates, maintaining a rigid silence until they reached Hanover Square. He helped her to alight, gave her a stiff bow, and said awfully, 'I doubt if we shall meet again, Miss Goodham.'

She gave him a contrite look. 'Forgive me, Your Grace. I did not mean to insult your mistress.'

'Miss Goodham.' He looked at her for a moment, outraged, and then jumped into his carriage and drove off.

'You did *what*?' exclaimed Pamela later that day when Honoria described her drive with the duke. 'Honoria, you *never* mention a man's mistress. We do not know of such women. For us they do not exist. How *could* you?'

'Perhaps it was very bad of me,' said Honoria contritely. 'He is a very disturbing man, and it is just as well I shall not be seeing him again.'

But Honoria had forgotten that the duke was to be present at the Buchans' turtle dinner.

The duke had always considered petty malice a character defect of lesser mortals. He had found out that the Buchans believed Miss Goodham to be an heiress because of one of Mr Delaney's ill-considered remarks, and when he met Lord Buchan in White's, he suddenly found himself saying, 'I believe Miss Goodham is to be a guest at supper on Saturday.'

'Yes, indeed, the most beautiful and charming young lady to visit London for some time. Archie is smitten, you know, and he has our blessing.'

'I am so glad your son is not so mercenary as most of society,' said the duke. 'It wearies me the way any heiress is automatically considered beautiful.'

'But that cannot be said of Miss Goodham,'

pointed out Lord Buchan. 'She *is* beautiful.'

'Although not an heiress.' The minute his words were out, the duke regretted them.

'But it is well known she is!'

Now was the time to draw back, but some imp goaded the duke on. 'Miss Goodham is from a good but provincial family of the gentry. A teasing remark by my friend, Mr Delaney, I fear, was what started the gossip.'

Lord Buchan fidgeted nervously. 'Dear, dear. Excuse me, Ware. Pressing business, pressing business.' He strode off, and the duke looked after him ruefully.

He sat down and tried to read the newspapers but he found he could not concentrate. This was ridiculous. He was becoming boring and middle-aged. He had behaved like a monk since he had come to London. Time to visit the much-neglected Penelope. He half rose, but sank back in his chair as Mr Delaney came into the coffee room.

'You are looking very happy,' commented the duke.

'I have been calling on my angel.'

'Mrs Perryworth? My friend, I find it hard to believe that you are out to seduce a vicar's wife.'

'Not I! Heaven forbid. I have stopped my nonsense. We have agreed on friendship.'

'Who are you fooling? Yourself or her? That is the oldest deception in the game.'

He walked out. He was angry with himself. But guilt was an emotion foreign to his nature, and so he did not recognize it for what it was.

* * *

The hour getting ready for the Buchans' turtle dinner was to remain in Honoria's mind for some time as her last period of happy innocence in London. So far the gossip and scandalous affairs of London society had passed her by. She sunnily believed the best of everyone. Why, even the wicked Duke of Ware was nothing more than a respectable middle-aged man who had chosen to befriend them. Mr Delaney had called that day. Pamela had told her about his offer of friendship, and there certainly was no longer anything in the Irishman's behaviour toward her friend to occasion either worry or comment.

She did not know that Mr Delaney had confided in Pamela that he was sure Archie Buchan's interest in Honoria was strictly mercenary, because Pamela had decided not to tell Honoria. There would be plenty of other men glad to wed her for her looks alone. Honoria, decided Pamela, had not the sophistication to know how to treat such a situation. If she continued in happy innocence, then she would behave at the dinner just as she ought.

Had she known that Honoria was

pleasurably enjoying her first romantic dreams, the subject being Archie, Pamela would have warned her. But Honoria had such an *untouched* air about her it was hard to imagine any thoughts running through that brain other than very unworldly ones. Perhaps Honoria would have remained heart-free had she not started reading novels. She had picked up one of Pamela's with a view to pointing out to her friend the folly of the writing and then had been completely lost in a fantasy world. As she read, the hero began to look more and more like Archie Buchan.

So, fresh and scented and happy, both set out for the Buchans' home, little aware of what was waiting for them.

Lady Buchan, alarmed at her dreadful mistake in cultivating Miss Goodham, had thought of cancelling the dinner, but on calmer reflection realized that with the duke to be present at her table as a lure, she could increase the dinner party to include two genuine heiresses, namely a Miss Briggs and a Miss Faring, and their parents. Archie was told firmly but sadly that they had been mistaken in Miss Goodham. She was not an heiress, and in any case, any female under the protection of Lady Dacey should not be encouraged. Archie sunnily accepted his parents' remarks and promised to court either Miss Faring or Miss Briggs like the dutiful son he was.

The company was gathered in the Buchans'

drawing room when Pamela and Honoria entered. Archie, Honoria saw immediately, was standing by the fireplace talking to two ladies. He looked up briefly at her and then returned to his conversation.

'So kind of you to come,' said Lady Buchan. 'Is Lady Dacey not yet returned?'

'No, I am afraid not,' said Pamela. She had noticed Archie's indifference and her heart sank. She wished now that she had warned Honoria.

'That must put you in a very difficult situation,' said Lady Buchan. 'Come and meet the rest of the company. Miss Briggs and Miss Faring...' And so the introductions went on. Honoria curtsied to Archie and thanked him shyly for the bouquet of flowers he had sent her that day. He gave her a hunted look, said hurriedly it was nothing, nothing at all, and then immediately engaged Miss Briggs in conversation again, talking about people Honoria did not know and therefore excluding her from the conversation.

The duke arrived with Mr Delaney just in time to see what was happening. He bowed to his hosts and walked immediately to Honoria's side and raised her hand to his lips. 'Miss Goodham,' he said in a caressing voice. 'Your beauty eclipses us all. Walk with me for a little. I have news of your aunt.'

'What news?' asked Honoria. She felt miserable about Archie. He had a silly laugh, she decided suddenly. She looked up at the duke, who smiled intimately down into her eyes, making her feel awkward and breathless.

'I heard from a friend recently returned from Paris that your aunt, Lady Dacey, had declared her intention of returning home to take up her duties, namely you and Mrs Perryworth.'

Honoria felt that what had started as a bad evening was becoming horrible. She realized all at once how comfortable she and Pamela were together and how she secretly dreaded her aunt's return. But there was worse to come. 'Do not take Archie Buchan's defection to heart,' she heard the duke say. 'I fear I am responsible for that. Mr Delaney put it about that you were an heiress. I disabused Lord Buchan of that notion. Hence the presence of two genuine heiresses and the busy courtship of Archie.'

'This is dreadful,' exclaimed Honoria. 'Such vanity! Mine, I mean. I am grateful to you, Your Grace, for interceding on my behalf. If Mr Buchan's interest in any female is because of her fortune, then he is not worth knowing.' She looked up at him candidly. 'And I know you are flirting with me to be kind, to give me a social cachet I might not otherwise have. I have heard you have a wicked reputation, but I judge people as I find them. It gives me pleasure to tell you, Your Grace, that I think you have a heart of gold.'

And the Duke of Ware blushed for the first time in his life.

Mr Delaney was furious with Archie Buchan. He felt the man should at least have tried to disguise his blatant greed. So just before they were about to go in for dinner, he murmured to Lady Buchan, 'It is wicked of Ware to put about that Miss Goodham is not an heiress.'

'What can you mean?' demanded Lady Buchan.

'I fear Ware has fallen in love at last.' Mr Delaney sighed. 'Miss Goodham is a considerable heiress, but by telling everyone that she is not, Ware hopes to cut down the competition.'

'Indeed! How odd!' Lady Buchan realized with anguish that she had placed Honoria at the bottom of the table, far away from Archie. She glared at Archie, who had relented enough to compliment Honoria on her gown.

Archie took that glare as a reminder that he was to forget Miss Goodham and so he added hurriedly, 'Of course, I do not know about such things as gowns. You must not take me seriously. Ah, I must take the beautiful Miss Briggs in to dinner.' He turned his back on Honoria and held out his arm to Miss Briggs. Lady Buchan stifled a groan.

Once they were all seated at the table, Lady Buchan noticed Honoria's downcast looks and cursed the Duke of Ware who, as the highest ranking guest, was seated next to her.

How to get a message to Archie? She had supplied the diners with those newfangled French table napkins. In most houses, the guests still wiped their mouths on the tablecloth. She waited until the duke was talking to the lady on his other side and taking a lead pencil out of her reticule, hurriedly scribbled the message, 'Miss Goodham IS an heiress,' on the starched linen surface of her napkin. She leaned forward to the duke. 'Would you be so good as to pass that to my son, Archie?'

The duke took the napkin, flipped it open, and glanced down at it just as the gentleman on Lady Buchan's other side claimed her attention. He took a lead pencil out of his pocket, and changed IS quickly to ISN'T, and told his neighbour to pass it to Archie.

Archie glanced down at the message and then up at his mother, who nodded to him solemnly. Archie was in awe of his domineering mother. He took the message to mean that he had not disaffected Miss Goodham properly enough and so during the meal, he flirted assiduously with Miss Briggs and Miss Faring, who were placed on either side of him.

When the ladies retired to the drawing room, Lady Buchan set out to be charming to Miss Goodham. Honoria began to relax and to think kindly of Archie again. But as soon as the gentlemen joined them, Archie went straight to Miss Briggs and Miss Faring and continued flirting.

'Now, why did Lady Buchan try to tell her son that Miss Goodham was an heiress after all?' the duke asked Mr Delaney.

'Because I told her you only said she was not because you wanted her for yourself,' replied Mr Delaney cheerfully.

'I should call you out. Do you know Lady Buchan wrote a message on a napkin that said Miss Goodham IS an heiress and asked me to send it along to Archie? I changed the IS to ISN'T, so our Archie is still being cold to Miss Goodham. Ah, his stern mama has his ear at last. Watch this.'

The duke quickly crossed to Honoria's side. 'Have you heard the latest *on-dit*, Miss Goodham? It seems that Lady Arthur, married only a month, took off for foreign parts with her first footman. Her husband pursued the guilty pair to Dover and fought the footman on the quayside. They beat each other nearly to a pulp and then retired to the nearest inn to have their wounds dressed while Lady Arthur fainted and sighed and fainted again, crying to all who would listen that two men were fighting over her, so there was little hope of keeping the matter quiet.

'Alas for Lady Arthur. When she awoke the next morning, feeling like Cleopatra and Delilah rolled into one, she was informed by her maid that her husband and the footman had become the best of friends and had gone abroad together.'

'That is very shocking,' said Honoria seriously. 'Poor Lady Arthur.'

'Poor nothing! She cuckolded her husband and made him fight with her lover as publicly as she possibly could.'

'I suppose other people's romances are considered ridiculous and funny,' said Honoria. 'But perhaps they are tragedies to the people concerned. What, for example, would you think if I told you that I was in love with Mr Archie and the fact he was spurning me was upsetting me greatly?'

'I would say you were a silly goose to waste your affections in that direction. But just in case you have formed a *tendre* for that worthless object who is now beaming on you—No! Walk with me, talk to me! He is not going to cut into our conversation. The fact of the matter is that Lady Buchan did believe you to be a great heiress. Disabused of the fact, she ordered Archie to be cool to you. Mr Delaney, in a spirit of mischief, told Lady Buchan that . . . that you were in fact an heiress after all and so she has no doubt ordered Archie to court you again.' The duke had no intention of telling Honoria that his friend had said he wanted her for himself.

'How sad and shabby all this is,' said Honoria. She turned away from him to face

Lady Buchan, who approached them with a beaming Archie in tow. 'Would you sing for us, Miss Goodham? My son would be delighted to turn the music for you.'

'Mrs Perryworth has a very fine voice,' said Honoria, avoiding Archie's gaze. 'You would find her the better choice. I am sorry. You were saying, Your Grace . . . ?'

'Now look what you have done, you idiot,' raged Lady Buchan as the duke led Honoria away. 'You have practically thrown her into Ware's arms.'

'Not my fault at all!' Archie looked hurt. 'You sent me that message at table saying she wasn't an heiress. You'd told me that already, so I thought you were giving me a further warning.'

'It said IS!'

'Is. Isn't. The damage is done for the moment. If I were you, Ma, I'd ask Mrs Perryworth to sing and therefore do something to please Miss Goodham.'

Pamela looked nervous when asked. She had never performed since her marriage, the vicar frowning on anything other than singing hymns in church. Honoria had heard her singing as she moved about Lady Dacey's house. It was one thing to sing when one was by herself, but another to perform in such fashionable company. Mr Delaney saw her confusion and said merrily, 'Come, Mrs Perryworth, we will give them a duet. I will play.'

He sat down at the piano and flicked through the music, after lighting the candles in their brackets on the pianoforte. 'Here we are.' His eyes glinted up at her mischievously in the candlelight. '"Oh, Love Divine," just the thing.' And before Pamela could protest, his fingers rippled expertly over the keys, and the guests fell silent.

The two voices rose and fell in the simple ballad, the soprano that was Pamela's voice intertwining with Mr Delaney's tenor.

Honoria, who had taken a seat next to the duke on a backless sofa, watched the couple uneasily. She felt they had forgotten everything in the world but each other, that they were singing the words to each other.

When they finished singing, the guests applauded enthusiastically and called for more, but Mr Delaney said quietly to Pamela, 'If only I could kiss you again.' Her colour flamed, and she walked away from the piano.

'I think he really is in love at last,' said the duke to Honoria. 'What a pity.'

'You must speak to him.' Honoria leaned toward the duke and spoke urgently. He was conscious of every bit of her, the way a tendril of brown hair lay against the cream of her cheek, the curve of her lips, the scent she wore. Without thinking, he took her hand and raised it to his lips. 'No, don't do that!' exclaimed Honoria, taking her hand away. 'I beg of you,

Your Grace, you must tell Mr Delaney to leave Pamela—I mean, Mrs Perryworth—alone.'

'It is not as easy as that,' he said. 'Love, once started, is very hard to stop. Archie is hovering about again. Talk to me about something, anything. I know—tell me about this vicar.'

'Oh, Mr Perryworth? Well, he is quite well-looking in his way. But a very cold man with a rather judgmental manner. "Mrs Perryworth, I trust you will behave becomingly in London and spurn the devil at all times."' He looked down at her in surprise, for she had mimicked the vicar's voice, he was sure, accurately. 'He delights in finding fault. Dear me, I am quite overset or I would not criticize the man so. But if only he were a warmer person, more *caring*, then perhaps Mrs Perryworth would not be in danger. Mr Delaney is very charming.'

'I am surprised Mr Perryworth allowed his wife to escape to London.'

'He is impressed by Lady Dacey's title and fortune, as are my parents. But he must miss her dreadfully. Mrs Perryworth does a great deal of the parish work.'

* * *

Mr Perryworth looked down on the heads of his congregation. He found his eyes fastening on a pretty bonnet decorated with red cherries, and with an effort tore his eyes away. The bonnet belonged to Mrs Sarah Watkins, a widow. She was a demure lady with a round rosy face, small black eyes, and very thick, glossy black hair. He had not noticed her particularly until one day when he had realized he had not called on her to welcome her to the parish, something that in the past he would have let his wife do for him.

He had knocked at her door. It had given under his knock. 'Mrs Watkins!' he called. He was used to walking in and out of the houses of his parishioners, for doors were hardly ever locked. He entered.

He found himself in a pretty parlour, but stopped short at the sight of Mrs Watkins herself, lying on a sofa near the window, asleep. Her black hair was loose and cascading about her white shoulders, which were revealed by a low-cut nightgown, all she was wearing. One leg was slightly raised with the thin material falling back from it.

He blushed and backed out, quietly closing the door behind him. But that vision of her stayed in his mind, burned into his memory. He felt his senses quickening when he thought of her in a way he knew he should not.

It was all his wife's fault, he thought angrily. Her letters were dull and correct with no particular news and no words of affection.

His eyes strayed back again to that fetching bonnet. At that moment, Mrs Watkins raised her head and gave him a slow, warm smile. He turned his eyes away again, but felt a glow of exultation that had nothing to do with religion.

CHAPTER SIX

Lady Dacey arrived back in London, unannounced, some three weeks later. She had initially had a pleasant time in Paris after she had got over her fury at learning that the Duke of Ware had not been seen anywhere in that city. She had been on the point of returning to London when fate had thrown a young charmer in the presence of one Guy Lupin in her path. He was twenty-three, lazy, and attractive. He professed himself devastated with her beauty, and for the first time in her life she had succumbed to the wiles of a young man who was only interested in her money. He deserted her for a younger, richer target on the same day as she read in an old copy of the *Morning Post* that the Duke of Ware had been seen driving Miss Honoria Goodham in the park.

She was in a very bad temper indeed and illogically blamed Honoria for having tricked her into going abroad. Only the thought of Honoria as she had last seen her, young and schoolgirlish, served to mollify her. Along with that came the thought that she had invited Honoria to London to use as bait. To have a young miss to bring out meant the company of eligible men. Lady Dacey planned to marry again and as soon as possible.

She arrived in the evening and was told that the ladies were at the opera with the Duke of Ware and Mr Delaney. The news made her bite her lip in a returning excess of fury.

She decided to wait up for them, tired as she was. After half an hour, she began to fret at the inaction and therefore resolved to change and visit the duke's box at the opera herself. Dressed in a new Parisian gown of violet silk and decked out in some of her finest jewels and with a feathered headdress, she set out.

Honoria was watching the opera, hands clasped, eyes shining, and the duke was watching Honoria. He was at times amused and at times irritated with the indifference with which she treated him. Little Miss Goodham, he thought wryly, was only using him while she looked about for someone younger and more interesting. There was one good thing. Although Archie Buchan still tried to court her, Honoria was barely civil to him. He knew she was contemptuous of a young man who was prepared to court only at his mother's bidding.

He studied Honoria's face and wondered idly if he could make her fall in love with him. The trouble was, he had never had to try to be particularly charming or civil to any female in his life before. His title and fortune had seen to that. Still, he might flirt with her a little to see how she coped with it.

He thought he would begin at the first interval by pressing her hand warmly as he led her from the box for the promenade in the corridor outside.

Mr Delaney and Pamela were sitting quietly, side by side. Although they were several inches apart, it was as if they were joined together, as if the one were thinking so intensely of the other that no one and nothing else mattered.

Mr Delaney was privately chafing at the bonds of friendship. He had been all that was correct, but he dreamed increasingly of what her lips had felt like under his own. He longed to reach out and take her hand. He was conscious at all times of every part of her body. A light-hearted love was sinking into a deep obsession, so that he felt as if he were tumbling down into a bottomless well of love with nothing to hold on to to stop him. He sometimes imagined what it would be like if he rode north and challenged the vicar to a duel.

And then just as the curtain descended at the first interval, the door to the box was flung open by an usher and Lady Dacey sailed in on a cloud of powerful scent.

'Aunt!' cried Honoria. Lady Dacey kissed her on the cheek and muttered, '*Don't call me that!*' before standing back to better survey her niece.

Her china blue eyes narrowed slightly as she took in the glory of that new crop, of the fresh and untouched beauty of that face, of the exquisite lines of a white muslin gown embroidered with rosebuds.

'I am glad you are returned, Clarissa,' said Pamela quietly. 'We were beginning to wonder if we would see you again.'

Lady Dacey ignored her and held out her hand to the duke. 'How do you do, Ware. Devastatingly handsome as ever.'

'And you are as beautiful as ever,' he said with automatic gallantry and kissed her hand.

'Naughty man!' She rapped him playfully with her fan. 'Do move over, Honoria, and let me sit next to Ware. I have not seen him this age.'

Honoria obediently took a chair on the far side of the box. Lady Dacey turned the chair on which Honoria had been sitting and sat down so that she was facing the duke while her back was to the rest of them.

Lady Dacey talked and flirted and told all the gossip of Paris. When the duke tried to glance past her to see what Honoria was doing, Lady Dacey had a way of quickly moving her head so that his view of the girl was blocked. At first he felt frustrated. Then he began to wonder if young Honoria could be made to feel jealous. So he capped Lady Dacey's outrageous stories with a few of his own.

But when the opera began again, Lady Dacey talked on and he could sense Honoria's irritation. He knew she was unfashionable enough to like to listen to the music and that by continuing to entertain her aunt, he was falling rapidly in her esteem.

By the end of the opera, Lady Dacey was almost purring like a cat. Honoria had fulfilled her role by bringing this wicked and handsome duke into Lady Dacey's own orbit.

Her delight intensified when the duke took her up to dance first at the opera ball. Honoria, whose reputation as heiress was already established, was immediately surrounded by courtiers.

'Let us sit and watch the dancers,' Mr Delaney urged Pamela. 'Yes, I know you are popular, too, but just for once say you are feeling faint.'

Pamela would normally have protested that such behaviour was neither correct nor fitting in a chaperon, but her feelings were thrown in a turmoil by the return of Lady Dacey and by the fact that the duke seemed to have forgotten Honoria's very existence. Pamela felt a pang of regret. She had begun to warm to the duke because of his kindness, his humour, and his courtesy. She had even begun to believe that his wicked days were over and that perhaps he might make Honoria a good husband.

But now she had only to look at the duke flirting expertly with the outrageous Lady Dacey to guess that he deserved every bit of his reputation, and so she refused her first partner and therefore was left free to sit quietly in a corner with Mr Delaney.

'Faith, this changes things,' said Mr Delaney, nodding in the direction of the duke and Lady Dacey. 'I can only hope your young friend is heart-free.'

'I am sure she is,' replied Pamela.

But Honoria found she was disturbed by the return of her aunt. The short time she had spent with the duke, Mr Delaney, and Pamela had kept her protected and innocent of the darker side of society. Lady Dacey and the duke seemed to share a world of wicked experience that she did not know and did not want to know. She realized with a little shock that she was once more under authority—that marriage was her duty. With a new ease she had acquired since she first came to London, however, she chatted to her partners and tried to block the duke from her mind. When she eventually found him standing before her asking for a dance, she blinked at him as if trying to bring him into focus.

'A waltz,' he said, smoothly guiding her steps. 'We should always dance the waltz together, you and I. Our steps match so well. Are you enjoying yourself?'

'Yes, Your Grace. I am delighted you have found a soul mate.'

He held her hand more tightly and smiled down at her. 'I am glad you have noticed it.'

'I think all must notice how well you and my aunt get along together.'

For one moment, his eyes darkened with anger and his clasp on her hand loosened. Then he gave a light laugh and said, 'Lady Dacey is certainly amusing.'

He looked across the ballroom. Lady Dacey was not dancing. She was talking to Lord Herne, not in her usual flirtatious way, but intently, seriously. He thought with a stab of alarm that it looked like a business meeting and hoped Honoria was not the trade they were dealing in. But then, what was this innocent girl to him? It had amused him, surely nothing else, to take her about. Now that Lady Dacey had returned, there was no need for him to do more. He could return to his own life.

When they promenaded after the waltz was over, Honoria found she was waiting for him to make some arrangement to see her again. He usually suggested something—a call, a drive in the park, a night at the opera—but as her next partner approached, he merely bowed and turned on his heel, leaving her feeling strangely flat.

She tried not to watch him, tried not to notice that he asked Lady Dacey for a second dance, or that this time, whatever he was saying to Lady Dacey was putting her in a bad mood. After that dance with Lady Dacey, she saw him stopping to exchange a few words with Pamela and Mr Delaney, and then he left the ballroom.

He had served his purpose, she told herself

firmly, trying to feel worldly-wise. He had done his best to bring her into fashion. But after she curtsied to her partner, she saw Lady Dacey approaching with Lord Herne and felt that as the duke had warned her against this man, he should have stayed to protect her.

'I am delighted you have already made the acquaintance of my good friend, Lord Herne,' said Lady Dacey. 'Herne begs a dance with you.'

Honoria stifled a sigh and curtsied. All these curtsies, bobbing up and down all evening when all she wanted to do was go home.

It was another waltz. So much for the fickle duke saying they should always waltz together. Lord Herne danced very well. She glanced up at him fleetingly. She supposed he could be accounted handsome, although his brooding, rather reptilian stare was a trifle unnerving.

After this dance, supper was served and Lord Herne escorted her to the supper room and sat beside her. 'Are you enjoying your first Season?' he asked.

'Yes, very much,' replied Honoria politely.

'It will be your first and your last.'

'Why so?'

'With your beauty, you will be engaged to be married by the end of it . . . or perhaps before it has begun.'

'You flatter me, my lord.'

He took a little painted chicken-skin fan out of his pocket and waved it languidly in the air.

'Not I. You have beauty to break hearts. You are fortunate to have such a sterling lady as Lady Dacey to bring you out.'

'Lady Dacey is all that is kind.'

'Lady Dacey has your best interests at heart. Perhaps she has not yet warned you about Ware.'

'There is nothing to warn me about. His Grace was merely being kind to someone considerably younger than he,' said Honoria with rare malice, judging Lord Herne to be about the same age as the duke.

'Ware is never kind. He pursues women and then leaves them. Ah, his poor mistress, cruelly abandoned.'

'I am sure his lawyers arranged an adequate settlement,' snapped Honoria. 'Such is usually the case, although I am sure you have more knowledge of such matters than I.'

'My dear Miss Goodham, allow me to be your guide. One does not mention such subjects in polite society.'

'Then in future, my lord, I suggest you do not bring them into the conversation.'

'We must not quarrel.' His odd eyes caressed her body in a way she did not like. 'I shall call on you tomorrow.'

'I regret, my lord, that I believe I have several calls to make.'

'On the contrary, Lady Dacey herself invited me and gave me permission to take you driving in the park.'

Honoria looked around for Pamela. She felt threatened. Her life was being organized for her. From now on, she would meet only the gentlemen Lady Dacey allowed her to meet. She would probably never see the duke again.

Fortunately for her, Lady Dacey discovered how tired she really was from her journey shortly after the duke left, and so she appeared to tell Honoria they were returning home.

Pamela was as silent as Honoria on the road back to Hanover Square. She felt a great weight of guilt somewhere in the pit of her stomach. She was letting herself fall more deeply in love every day. And yet she found it in her heart to be concerned for Honoria. It was almost as if the pair of them had been plunged back into their old life of thralldom overnight. While they had been waiting at the opera for Lady Dacey's carriage to be brought round, Honoria had protested that she did not really want to go driving on the following day with Lord Herne, to which Lady Dacey had replied calmly, 'You will do as you are told.'

When they entered the house, Lady Dacey said to Pamela, 'I would have a word with you in private. Go to bed, Honoria.'

In the Green Saloon, Lady Dacey said briskly, 'Delaney is in love with you and you are encouraging him.'

Pamela looked at the floor and said in a stifled voice, 'I am sorry if that is the way it appears. Mr Delaney is a good friend and . . .'

'Good friend, fiddlesticks. Harken to me, Pamela. You have done well in my absence. You have attired young Honoria in style, although I thought her braids were pretty. Never mind. Herne is interested in her and would make her a good husband.'

'Never!'

Lady Dacey's voice was like silk. 'You will help me to secure Herne for Honoria or I will write to that husband of yours and suggest he travel south to see how you go on with Sean Delaney.'

'That will not be necessary,' said Pamela with cold contempt. 'For I shall not be seeing Mr Delaney again, so you may not use that as a weapon.'

'You shouldn't try to cross me. Your usefulness is over. Pack and get ready to leave in the morning. I shall go and tell Honoria so.'

Honoria looked up as her aunt entered the room. 'I have just told Pamela to take her leave in the morning.'

'Why?' Honoria put down the hairbrush she had been holding.

'Because she dared to cross me. She is behaving scandalously with Delaney. I think Herne is a good catch for you. Pamela protested. So I told her I would tell that husband of hers about Delaney. So she gets uppity and says she will not see Delaney again.'

Honoria sat very still. She wondered briefly why her aunt's behaviour was not surprising.

Then she said with an affected calm, 'That indeed is very sad, for in that case I must return as well. Oh, I will be beaten for it and forced to marry a local man whom I detest and Papa will have to pay you for all my clothes. But I will not see my friend sent away in this humiliating way.' She turned back to the mirror and picked up the brush again. 'One last favour, Clarissa. I will write a letter to the Duke of Ware. He will be monstrous sad that we are leaving, as will his friend. Of course, as he has been all that is kind, I will explain my reasons for leaving.'

'Minx! I shall not deliver such a letter!'

'Then Pamela and I will call at the duke's townhouse and deliver it in person. And now, Clarissa, all that remains is for me to thank you for your hospitality. I will also tell Papa and Mama that we had to rely on the duke and Mr Delaney for our social entrée, as you were in Paris.'

'Now, now, turn around again and pay attention to me,' said Lady Dacey, sitting down heavily on the bed and staring at her niece. 'Let me think.'

She sat, scowling horribly, while Honoria watched her with outward calm and inner turmoil. Surely her aunt would not do anything to disaffect the Duke of Ware.

'I cannot believe such a sermon-reading widgeon as yourself,' said Lady Dacey at last, 'could be capable of such guile. But it looks to me as if you are telling me that without you and the vicar's wife, Ware won't call. Well, let me tell you, Miss Milksop, that Ware could hardly bear to be away from my side this evening.'

Lady Dacey gave her a calculating look but Honoria said, her lips curling with amusement, 'Oh, *I* thought he was being courteous to you because of *me*.'

'Why should he bother about a tepid young miss like you?'

'Dear me, *I* don't know, I am sure, but while you were away, he called almost every day. Of course, the minute he learns you mean to hand me over to Herne—and that is what you plan, is it not?—I am sure he will stay clear and believe me, *Aunt*, he certainly will not call if Pamela and I are not in residence.'

Lady Dacey stood up, and as she did so, she saw her own tired face reflected in the mirror and then looked at Honoria's beautiful one. Then there had been that lecture that Ware had given her before he left the ballroom. He had told her to do her best for Honoria and that 'best' should not include trying to affiance her to a lecher like Herne. But rich as Lady Dacey was, she adored jewels, and Herne had promised her the Light of India, a huge diamond on display at the famous jewellers, Rundell and Bridge's, if she let him have Honoria.

She looked up, for Honoria had begun to speak again. Honoria had suddenly wondered if she could begin the reformation of her aunt by guile rather than by sermonizing. 'It has been my observation, Clarissa,' she said, 'that ladies who dress like women of easy virtue are treated as such.'

'Are you referring to me, you impertinent baggage!'

'I am only saying that the immodesty of your dress belies the fact that you are a great lady with a good heart who wishes to marry again and yet must advertise to the world at large that perhaps favours can be got outside marriage.'

'And how do you know all this, Miss Innocent?'

'By observation. As you were not present, Pamela and I put our time to good use by listening to *on-dits*, by studying the lords and ladies, to put it crudely, by studying the *market*. A good woman weds: a bad woman does not.'

Instead of being furious—which she really felt she ought to be—Lady Dacey was struck by this novel idea. What was the point of having men lust after you instead of falling in love with you? And that Pamela Perryworth had an exquisite dress sense.

She was sure if she could spend some more time in Ware's company, she could secure him. Honoria's prattle, that of a young girl, would soon bore him.

Everyone at the ball had been commenting on Honoria's beauty. Young men flocked round her. Instead of sending their servants to present their compliments the next day, Lady Dacey was sure that the gentlemen who had danced with Honoria would call in person. There was nothing, she felt, more delightful, more exhilarating than to be in a room full of men. Yes, she had to accept the wisdom of Honoria's remarks. She liked to shock; she enjoyed scandalizing the more sober matrons of society with her outrageous gowns. But outrageous gowns were not going to get her to the altar again. Ware was looking for a *duchess*, not a trollop.

Honoria watched her, her heart beating hard, praying inwardly to God to forgive her for scheming in such a way as to stay in London.

To her immense surprise, Lady Dacey sighed and said, 'What think you of the wig?'

Honoria looked at the red wig.

She said cautiously, 'Red hair is not fashionable. I have never seen your own hair.'

Lady Dacey whipped off the wig, and revealed a cropped head of black curls.

'Why, your own hair is vastly pretty, Aunt. It makes your eyes look monstrous large.' Privately Honoria thought that her aunt was one of those rare women whose eyes could do with being reduced in size. 'Perhaps, Aun—I mean Clarissa—I could tell Pamela we are staying, after all?'

'Yes, yes. You must forgive my tetchiness,

my dear. I am overset after the journey.'

Honoria smiled sweetly. 'I shall go now and see Pamela and then I shall read to you.'

Lady Dacey groaned but Honoria was already leaving the room.

Pamela was packing her clothes, only the clothes she had brought with her, tears dropping on the fabric.

'Dry your eyes,' said Honoria. 'You are not going.'

'Why? What happened?'

Honoria related her conversation with her aunt. Pamela looked at her in amazement. 'I would never have believed you could be so ... so devious, Honoria.'

'Needs must,' said Honoria with a little shrug. 'I could not contemplate staying in London without you. But to return *now*! Papa and Mama would be furious and we do not want Aunt writing anything about Mr Delaney to Mr Perryworth.'

'Not that there is anything to write about,' said Pamela defiantly, although a glow of sheer relief and happiness was spreading inside her. If Lady Dacey were to pursue Ware, that meant seeing more of Ware's friend instead of the agony of avoiding him altogether.

'Put those clothes of yours back in the press, dear,' said Honoria, 'or burn them, for you will now be able to take your new clothes home to dazzle the county of Yorkshire.' She looked at Pamela and a crusading light lit up her eyes.

'And now I am going to read to Aunt.'

'I am glad I threw that book of sermons out of the window,' commented Pamela, 'for she would certainly not enjoy hearing those.'

'I have my Book of Common Prayer,' said Honoria.

* * *

Lady Dacey shifted uneasily in bed as Honoria sat down primly on a hard chair beside it and opened a large volume of the Book of Common Prayer. 'Is this necessary, my dear?' asked Lady Dacey faintly.

'An evening psalm is always necessary,' said Honoria and began to read Psalm 137.

' "By the waters of Babylon we sat down and wept: when we remembered thee, O Sion.

' "As for our harps, we hanged them up: upon the trees that are therein.

' "For they that led us away captive required of us then a song, and melody, in our heaviness: Sing us one of the songs of Sion.

' "How shall we sing the Lord's song: in a strange land?

' "If I forget thee, O Jerusalem: let my right hand forget her cunning.

' "If I do not remember thee, let my tongue cleave to the roof of my mouth: yea, if I prefer not Jerusalem in my mirth.

' "Remember the days of Edom, O Lord, in the day of Jerusalem: how they said, Down with it, down with it, even to the ground.'"

A faint snore came from the bed. Lady Dacey was fast asleep. Honoria looked down at her sleeping aunt with something approaching love. There was always hope for reform.

It was only when she reached her own bedroom that she realized that London had changed her, had made her much braver than she had ever been before. Lord Herne? Pooh! There was nothing he could do. She could not be constrained to marry him, or anyone, not anymore. Freedom from home should not lie in the hands of some future husband. She stood frowning. She had had a good education. Despite what she had heard, she was sure she could find employ as a governess, although being so young she would find it difficult to obtain such a position. But if she and Pamela joined forces to start a school! If they could find a little money to do that! But that would be taking Pamela away from her husband, and that would be a wicked thing to do.

* * *

Mr Perryworth had finished his rounds of the village. He had an urge to call on Mrs Watkins, just to be civil, but when he knocked at her door, there was no reply, and he could not find the courage to open the door and look into the parlor and see whether she was at home or not.

The day was fine, and daffodils were blowing in the tussocky grass of the churchyard and a forsythia bush spilled its golden glory over a mossy table tombstone. A marble angel held one pale finger up to the pale blue sky. The vicar was reluctant to return to the empty vicarage and walked back out onto the road and so out of the village toward the moors, unconsciously following the path taken by his wife when she wished to escape from the constraints of her marriage.

He rounded a bend in the road and stopped short. Mrs Watkins was in the act of mounting a stile, her skirts hitched up, showing a well-turned ankle. The blustery wind was moulding her clothes against her body. He experienced an odd feeling near to panic and was about to turn about when she called, 'Mr Perryworth! Can you help me, please?'

He went forward to join her. Her eyes glinted down at him. 'Could you help me, please, sir?'

'Gladly.'

'My skirt appears to have caught on a splinter and I do not want to pull at it.'

Annoyed to find himself blushing, he found that the silk skirt of her dress had become caught on a splinter sticking out of a post on the stile. He gently detached it and stood back.

'Thank you,' she said demurely, making to step down from the stile, and then she swayed toward him. He automatically put out his arms and caught her. He was suddenly, violently aware of her body pressed against his own, of the musky animal smell emanating from her, of the way she was smiling up at him, and of how thick and *juicy* her lips looked, like ripe berries.

He set her away from him and then babbled, 'You must excuse me, ma'am. I have an urgent letter to write to my wife.'

She stood in the road, her hands on her hips, and watched him go. He did not know it, but she had seen him coming along the road from a vantage point up on the moor and had hurried down to that stile and stabbed her good silk gown onto that splinter just as he rounded the bend. She smiled slowly and then began to walk along the road in the direction he had taken.

* * *

The Duke of Ware had just finished tying his cravat when Mr Delaney, who was allowed to come and go as he pleased in the duke's house, strolled into the room. 'Getting ready to come with me?' he asked.

'Where?' asked the duke. 'The club?'

'You are singularly obtuse today, my friend. To call on our ladies, to be sure.'

'*Your* ladies, perhaps. I have been very kind—for me—to Miss Goodham. I shall send my servant with my card and compliments.'

'But I cannot go on my own!'

'Without me for cover? Go and talk to Mrs Perryworth yourself.'

'Considering that you danced with Honoria as well as Lady Dacey last night, I thought you might wish to call in person.'

'Honoria? You are grown familiar.'

'She is like a child to me. Oh, say you will come. Herne will be there, no doubt.'

'I have already warned Lady Dacey about encouraging Herne.'

'And you think she will listen to you? That one? Come, think of Honoria clasped in Herne's arms.'

The duke turned back to the arrangement of his cravat. He said in a neutral voice, 'What Miss Goodham does with her future is no concern of mine. Oh, very well. If it pleases you, we will call, but only for a few moments.'

* * *

Lady Dacey was not pleased. She was wearing what she privately considered to be a frumpy gown. Herne had called, and was still present. Several charming young men had called, but there was no sign of Ware. Had she reduced herself to a dowd and all because of the machinations of a young provincial miss?

Herne finally took his leave. Honoria and Pamela had been chilly but correct. After Lord Herne had left the room, Lady Dacey faced her guests. 'Now, look here . . .' she began.

The double doors behind her opened again. 'His Grace, the Duke of Ware, and Mr Delaney,' announced her butler.

She swung round and held out both hands to the duke, who kissed them. 'Lady Dacey,' he said, standing back to look at the effect of real hair and modest gown, 'I have never seen you look better.'

All Lady Dacey's anger at Honoria and Pamela faded away. 'Come and be seated, gentlemen. Honoria, do play something to entertain us.'

She sat down on a sofa and patted the space next to her, but to her annoyance the duke crossed to the piano and said, 'Let me turn the pages for you.'

Honoria glanced up at him. She was wearing a pretty morning gown with a high neck and long sleeves, and yet he thought she looked outrageously seductive. 'Mrs Perryworth is the better musician,' said Honoria. 'I am but an indifferent performer.'

'Then let Mrs Perryworth entertain us,' cried Lady Dacey. 'No, I insist. Come and sit by me, Ware, and give me all the latest *on-dits*.'

Honoria surrendered the piano stool to Pamela. Mr Delaney took the duke's place.

Pamela played a Mozart sonata. Lady Dacey listened with amusement to the duke who was regaling her with the story of a certain young Mr Rigby's flighty opera dancer. And then, after the sonata was finished, Pamela and

Mr Delaney began to sing a love song. The duke fell silent. Lady Dacey tried to keep the conversation going, but he held up his hand for silence. Honoria sat with her head bowed, conscious of the underlying passion in the voices, sensing the duke's eyes on her, feeling breathless, ill at ease, and almost frightened, as if she had suddenly found herself standing on the brink of the unknown. As the voices twined and rose and fell, she raised her eyes and looked at the duke and he held her gaze for a long moment. Pamela struck the final chord. Lady Dacey applauded, but said quickly, 'Enough of singing.'

Pamela remained motionless at the piano with Mr Delaney, equally motionless, beside her. The duke was very still, his eyes now hooded, but turned in Honoria's direction, Honoria who sat like a beautiful statue with the quick rise and fall of her bosom the only movement about her.

'Honoria,' said Lady Dacey with a well-manufactured shudder, 'fetch my shawl. The blue and crimson one. 'Tis become cold. You will find it in the press in my bedchamber.'

Honoria obediently left the room. 'Tish!' exclaimed Lady Dacey. 'Do go after her, Pamela, and tell her to bring my bonnet and cloak.' When Pamela had gone out, Lady Dacey smiled at the duke. 'I long to take the air. Perhaps I can persuade you to take me for a drive.'

He opened his mouth to make some polite excuse, but then some imp prompted him to say he would be delighted, all because he wanted to see the look in Honoria's eyes when she heard he was squiring her aunt to the park.

Honoria and Pamela returned together. Lady Dacey stood up and smiled slowly. 'Help me on with my cloak, Honoria. Ware is taking me for a drive.'

Quickly, the duke looked at Honoria's face. She dropped her eyes to conceal her expression, but not before the piqued and angry duke had caught a look of pure relief.

CHAPTER SEVEN

Pamela and Honoria were alone again. 'What do you think of that?' asked Pamela.

'Ware taking Aunt for a drive?' replied Honoria. 'Not very much. They are well suited, I think.'

Pamela looked at her curiously. Had there been a slight edge in that clear voice?

But she said, 'Now that we have a little free time, I feel I must visit my sister. She does complain so of my neglect.' Pamela sighed. 'And yet when I go there, all she does is lie on the chaise longue in that darkened room with her eyes half-closed.'

'I will come with you,' said Honoria. She did

not want to sit there until Lady Dacey returned but refused to think of the reason why.

Pamela crossed to the writing desk. 'I will leave a note for Clarissa.' She scribbled a short message saying they had gone to Lincoln's Inn Fields to visit her sister.

They ordered the carriage to be brought round from the mews and changed into carriage dresses, Pamela thinking of the days not so long ago when one morning gown, and a very plain one, too, was expected to serve until evening.

Amy, Mrs Aspen, was at home. But then she always was. Honoria hated that dark sitting room of Amy's where the hostess lay on the chaise longue, a console table at her head containing an assortment of little medicine bottles and pill boxes.

'You are come at last,' said Amy faintly, one limp white hand waving them toward chairs. 'I was beginning to think the only news I would ever have of my own sister would be through the social columns. There is much talk of Miss Goodham here and the Duke of Ware.'

'Tittle tattle,' said Pamela. 'Lady Dacey is returned, and Ware has taken her driving.'

'Ah, well, *that* was only to be expected,' said Amy.

'Why?' demanded Honoria in a brittle voice. She could not understand her own feelings. She had been relieved when she had learned that he was to go out with her aunt, for she was beginning to feel strangely threatened by him, but the relief had gone and there was a sour aftertaste.

'Like to like,' said Amy languidly.

* * *

The duke returned with Lady Dacey and accepted her invitation to enter the house. He had decided that Honoria could not possibly have looked relieved. But Lady Dacey found the note immediately and said, 'They are gone to see her sister in Lincoln's Inn Fields.'

'I did not know she had a sister in London,' said the duke, thinking Lady Dacey meant Honoria.

'Yes, a Mrs Aspen in Lincoln's Inn Fields, hard by The White Stag. Now, some wine?'

'No, I thank you. I must leave.' He kissed her hand. Disappointed, Lady Dacey watched him go and then ran to the window and sighed romantically as she saw him climbing into his carriage. Such a paragon was too much of a man for a widgeon like Honoria.

The duke decided to drive to Lincoln's Inn Fields and see this sister of Honoria's. Perhaps the woman would turn out to be common and his visit would embarrass Honoria and quite rightly, too. Besides, he was curious to meet a member of this infuriating girl's family.

He inquired at The White Stag for the address of the Aspens. He did not pause to think what speculation his visit might provoke. Like most aristocrats, he was single-minded, and did not often stop to think about anything other than satisfying his curiosity.

Honoria was to remember for long afterward the almost ridiculous change in Amy Aspen when the Duke of Ware was announced. She let out a shriek and cried to the little maid, 'Keep him belowstairs for a moment. Fetch my green shawl. Draw back the curtains. Open the windows.'

With the energy of a young girl, she rose from the chaise longue, swept all the bottles and pills into a work basket, and slammed down the lid.

When the duke entered, Amy was standing by the fireplace, one hand on the marble shelf, wrapped in the green shawl and showing some vestiges of the prettiness she had once had.

'What brings you here?' demanded Honoria bluntly once the introductions had been made.

'I found I had time on my hands,' he said, feeling silly. 'I have just taken Lady Dacey for a drive.'

Amy rang the bell and ordered wine and cakes. Her cheeks were flushed and her eyes sparkling. In that moment, as he looked at her and recognized the family resemblance, the duke realized she was Mrs Perryworth's sister, not Honoria's, and felt even sillier. He covertly studied Honoria as Amy began to prattle London gossip that she had culled from magazines and newspapers. Honoria's face was shadowed by a Pamela bonnet, that wide brimmed straw hat that was still in fashion. The crown was decorated with white and gold flowers. Her carriage gown, worn under a pelisse, was of gold silk. Her long lashes veiled her eyes. She had taken off her gloves. Her small hands were white and well shaped. He wanted to take one of those ungloved hands in his own with such a sudden intensity that it surprised him.

He answered Amy automatically with the practised ease of a man used to being bored. When Amy at last paused for breath, Pamela asked him if he had enjoyed his drive. 'Yes, very much,' he said politely. He saw Honoria glance furtively at the clock on the wall and found himself adding, 'I found her delightful company. Do you go anywhere this evening?'

'To the opera,' replied Pamela. 'We really must leave, Amy.'

Amy made a moue of disappointment and then said gaily, 'No matter. I am refreshed by your visit. The next time I shall call on you.' Pamela and Honoria exchanged glances, each thinking the same thing. There was a social gulf between Lincoln's Inn Fields and Hanover Square. Rattle she might be, but both instinctively felt sure that any visit by Amy would be regarded as social presumption by Lady Dacey.

They all rose at once. The duke saw those

white hands reaching for the gloves. He crossed the room and seized Honoria's hands and raised them to his lips, kissing first one and then the other. Honoria's hands trembled lightly in his own and then she freed them and pulled on her gloves. Her eyes surveyed him candidly.

And then to Pamela's surprise, she heard Honoria say, 'I am glad you enjoyed your drive with my aunt. Mrs Aspen was just saying you and Lady Dacey are well suited.'

'How very true,' he said blandly, although he was suddenly furious. 'We are all in a matchmaking mood today. It must be the spring weather. I have almost decided that Lord Herne would do very well for you.'

'Surely not, Your Grace.' Honoria smiled up at him. 'So very *old*. Perhaps if you and Aunt do not suit, she might find Lord Herne a suitable partner.'

He had thought that when the time ever came that he should decide to get married, all he had to do was smile on some young creature for her to fall into his arms. He could hardly believe Honoria's behaviour.

'Will you be at the opera, Your Grace?' asked Honoria.

'No,' he said abruptly. 'I found it a trifle tedious the other night.'

'Oh, you must avoid tedious company at all costs,' said Honoria sweetly.

'I fully intend to from now on!'

To the devil with her, he thought as he drove off. A man of his rank and dignity was not going to make a fool of himself over a provincial chit who did not know what was due to his rank and consequence. He said as much later to Mr Delaney, whose eyes began to sparkle wickedly. 'Faith, you are grown pompous, Ware. You have just made it clear to Miss Goodham that you prefer the company of her saucy aunt. You tell her further that you found the company at the opera tedious, therefore, in effect, telling her *she* is tedious, and then, when she proves to be the better fencer, you go very stiffly on your stiffs. You'll be ordering me out of your house next. But I am grateful to you. I now know where to find them.'

'You are never going to the opera again!'

'Of course. My needs are simple. To sit next to her, to smell her scent, to hear the rustle of her gown, and the sound of her soft voice.' Mr Delaney leaned back in his chair and half-closed his eyes.

'How can such a notorious breaker of hearts as yourself become so spoony over a mere vicar's wife?'

'I don't know,' said Mr Delaney simply. 'I have this mad idea of riding north and begging the vicar to release her.'

'From the little I have heard of him, all that would achieve would be to have him post south and take a horsewhip first to his wife and then to you.'

Mr Delaney sighed. 'You have the right of it. Do you come to the opera with me?'

'No,' said the duke harshly. 'I am going to go out drinking and wenching and if you had any sense left in your besotted head, you would come with me.'

* * *

The vicar was attending a village concert, organized by the local squire, Sir John Cartwright, who had imported a conjurer from the nearest large town for the occasion. The conjurer had a rapt audience and was a great success. Then the village band performed several numbers, the choir sang hymns, and after that it was announced that Mrs Watkins would sing a ballad.

He found he was sitting forward in his seat with his hands clenched on his knees. She walked onto the small stage wearing a diaphanous white gown, her glossy black hair piled high on her head. Two men carried in a large gilt harp. Mrs Watkins sat down and began to accompany her singing on the harp. She sang an Irish ballad, sad and lilting, and the vicar sat like a man enchanted.

There was a reception at the squire's afterward. Mr and Mrs Goodham were there, carrying newspaper cuttings that contained mention of Honoria being accompanied to this and that by the Duke of Ware. Mr Perryworth listened with only half an ear, for Mrs Watkins was chatting to the squire and the squire was leering down the front of her gown.

'Excuse me,' he said abruptly and, cutting the Goodhams off in mid-sentence, he crossed to join Mrs Watkins and the squire.

'You are not drinking the squire's excellent punch,' cried Mrs Watkins, looking at the glass of lemonade in his hand.

'Our good vicar never touches anything stronger than lemonade, hey, vicar?' said the squire.

Mrs Watkin's eyes caressed the vicar. 'Oh,' she said softly, 'but it is such good punch.' She raised her own glass to her full red lips and took a sip.

'I *am* rather cold,' he said. 'Perhaps I will have a glass.'

The squire summoned a maid and told the girl to fetch the vicar a glass of punch.

The squire made very strong brandy punch indeed. The vicar somehow found himself in the bay of the window, drinking punch and listening to Mrs Watkins, who was telling him how her friends had always said her voice was good enough for opera. The spirits coursed through his veins, giving him a boldness he did not know he was capable of.

After several glasses of punch, when she said she must take her leave and that although her little house was not too far, she did not like walking home alone in the dark, he promptly offered to accompany her. Once outside, under the reeling stars, it seemed only natural to take her arm in his.

His steps faltered and staggered slightly but Mrs Watkins did not seem to notice, saying breathily that it was so marvellous to have a strong man to lean on. When a fox darted across the road, she let out such an endearing little cry and pressed her body close to his.

* * *

Lady Dacey was a model of correct dress that evening. By wearing two dresses, one of transparent muslin over one of silk, with a lacy fichu tucked into the low neckline, she felt she had achieved the necessary modesty of appearance to make her marriageable. She had protested to Honoria before they set out that she had managed to fascinate men in the past with her daring gowns, to which Honoria had replied bluntly, 'That was when you were younger.'

Lady Dacey would have been cheered had she known that Honoria privately thought her aunt was looking extremely attractive with her curling black hair in a short crop. Not only was her dress becoming, but her face was skilfully painted and, in the blaze of candlelight in the opera house, looked as delicate as a flower. Lord Herne was sharing their box. Honoria tried not to listen to his compliments, aware that Pamela appeared too absorbed in listening to Mr Delaney who had joined them to do her duty, namely stop Lord Herne from pestering her.

At the interval, Lady Dacey turned and called to Mr Delaney, 'Where is Ware? Does he join us?'

'He is set on wenching and drinking tonight, or so he told me.'

Lady Dacey glared accusingly at Honoria and then flicked a contemptuous glance at her own gown.

Oh, dear, thought Honoria, she will now decide that the only way to attract such a rake is by reverting to her old style and manner, and she may decide she would be better without Pamela and me. The spectre of Mr Pomfret loomed before her eyes. All her previous bravery, her determination to have a say in how she ran her own life, crumbled. She felt quite cross and weepy.

The curtain rose on the second act. It was a poor opera by an unknown Italian composer and the music could not banish her angry thoughts. What was the duke doing? If he was consorting with prostitutes then it was all too easy to imagine what he was doing. There were so many prostitutes in London, and so many in the opera house plying their wares, that it was very hard for even a respectable female to avoid knowing what went on.

She felt obscurely betrayed by the duke. Lord Herne had edged his chair so close to her own that she could feel the heat of his body and smell the powerful scent with which he had drenched himself. Her head began to ache. She began to wonder if, instead of the insipid, careful letters she had been writing home, she should not beg her parents to send for her. They were her parents, after all, and surely if she made a stand, they would not force her into an unwelcome marriage. But then she knew that her parents, like most other parents in Regency England, would consider it a deep disgrace to have an unmarried daughter. Spinsters were a source of pity mixed with dislike, failures on the stage of life.

She felt a treacherous stab of impatience with Pamela. She *had* a husband, although that seemed to be a fact that was slipping more and more from her mind. Mr Perryworth was a cold fish, but he did not beat her and she had a household of her own.

Honoria decided she would not think of Ware anymore, and when she saw him again—*if* she saw again—she would demonstrate to him by her very coldness just how little he had been in her thoughts.

* * *

The duke was playing hazard at his club. He had drunk a great deal without any of it seeming to lift his spirits. Any time he thought of Honoria, he felt weary. Silly little chit, he told himself. Later that evening, he would go to a Cyprian ball at the Argyle Rooms and meet some *real* women. He realized all he had drunk was beginning to affect him when he began to lose heavily. But he was one of that rare breed of aristocrat who was determined not to pass his gaming losses onto his tenants, and so he left the tables.

Outside the club, the sooty acrid smell of London caught him by the throat. His carriage, with coach man on the box and footmen standing by the open door, waited patiently for his instructions.

'Opera house,' he said curtly, and climbed inside.

Twice on the road there, he rose to call to the coachman to take him to the Argyle Rooms but each time changed his mind and sank back in his seat.

At the opera house he avoided the blandishments of the prostitutes with practised ease. From the buzz of conversation emanating from the house, he gathered the opera was not a popular one.

He entered Lady Dacey's box.

Honoria heard the door of the box being opened, then Lady Dacey's cry of, 'Ware! How good of you to join us.'

The air about Honoria suddenly felt charged with electricity, as if before a thunderstorm.

She kept her eyes fixed on the stage. She could hear the rapid murmur of her aunt's voice behind her and then the duke's answering laugh.

Pamela glanced anxiously at Honoria. Love had sharpened all her senses, and she knew in that moment that Honoria was upset by the duke's conversation with Lady Dacey. She hoped that Honoria would not do anything silly, like encouraging the attentions of Lord Herne in order to retaliate.

All Pamela could think of when the opera ended was the ball ahead. Lady Dacey's box was crowded at the end of the performance by young men, all paying court to Honoria. Some of them were very attractive, but Pamela was sure that Honoria did not really notice any of them and cursed the day when their carriage had overturned in that snowstorm. All her own fears of divine retribution came back. She herself was behaving disgracefully and every sin had its price. She bowed her head as if a weight had been put upon it.

At the ball, Honoria granted Lord Herne the first dance with every evidence of delight, and the duke danced with Lady Dacey. Pamela accepted her first partner with relief; relief at getting away from Mr Delaney for a short time, Mr Delaney with his Irish charm, Mr Delaney who made her heart beat so quickly.

'I believe Honoria entertained you when she stayed at your hunting box by reading you sermons,' said Lady Dacey before twirling gracefully under the duke's arm.

'It was very . . . er . . . reforming,' he said with a smile.

'The dear girl started reading the psalms to me the other night, but fortunately I fell asleep.'

'Which should all go to show you that Herne is not the man for her,' said the duke.

'I think you are wrong. He is ready to settle down and mend his ways, and only see how Honoria smiles at him.'

The duke had a sudden desire to wring Honoria's slim white neck. Herne had a brooding, predatory look in his eyes. He wondered if Honoria knew she had no choice. Lord Herne was rich and influential. Lady Dacey would give her permission to a marriage and then write to Honoria's parents, who would be relieved that their daughter had secured such an eligible catch. Any protestations on her part about the character of the man would be ignored. He had seen many young misses standing red-eyed before the altar at their fashionable weddings.

He wondered whether it was his own vanity speaking to him or whether Honoria was being particularly pleasant to Lord Herne in order to get even with him for courting her aunt. He began to flirt outrageously with Lady Dacey. When he took her into supper, he noticed out of the corner of his eye that Honoria had accepted Herne's invitation and was sitting chatting to him in a flushed and animated way quite unlike her usual cold poise.

Pamela grew increasingly unhappy about her own situation. Honoria needed her help and her full-time concentration. 'Mr Delaney,' she began. He looked at her intently, noticing the sadness in her eyes. 'I have enjoyed our friendship, but even that must come to an end. No, let me speak. People will gossip so. Lady Dacey already has threatened to write to Honoria's parents about us. Besides, I am in London solely as Honoria's chaperon and must set her a good example and devote all my time to her.'

She had spoken in a low voice. They were surrounded by people. It was not the place to exclaim or protest. He would need to agree and then think furiously about what to do. So he said quietly, 'As you will,' and Pamela forced a smile as she felt the bottom dropping out of her world. There was some small comfort. She had done the right thing. Now all she had to do was to wait for the pain of loss to go away.

After supper Honoria danced until her feet ached. She danced the waltz with Lord Herne, remembering that the duke had said they should always waltz together. *He* was waltzing with a buxom blonde and looked as if he were enjoying every minute of it. Perhaps Lady Dacey had noticed his enjoyment for after the waltz was over, she announced that they should go home.

When they arrived at Hanover Square in the gray dawn, Honoria, on alighting from the carriage saw the duke's carriage pulling up as well. 'I have invited Ware to take tea with us,' said Lady Dacey, 'but I am sure you are both too fatigued to join us.' This was delivered in the manner of a command rather than a statement.

Pamela and Honoria said goodnight to the duke in the hall and made their way upstairs. 'What a night!' said Honoria, sinking down into a chair in her room. 'If I feel exhausted now, think what it will be like when the Season begins.'

Pamela took a seat opposite her and said, 'I have told Mr Delaney our friendship must end. I cannot risk Lady Dacey writing to Yorkshire. I have been neglecting my duties as your chaperon.'

Honoria looked at Pamela's sad face and wondered what to say. Pamela had done just as she ought, but on the other hand, when the Season was over, she had the rest of her life to face with the chilly vicar.

'You were encouraging Lord Herne tonight,' said Pamela.

Honoria looked away and said lightly, 'It is the fashion to flirt.'

'There are many young and eligible men interested in you.'

'Such as Archie Buchan? They are probably

all courting me because they believe me to be an heiress.'

'Nonetheless, it is dangerous to encourage such a man as Herne.'

'Pooh, go to bed, Pamela. I am well able to take care of myself.'

But when Pamela had left, Honoria paced restlessly up and down, trying not to think of the duke and Lady Dacey alone in the drawing room. She realized she was very hungry. She had eaten very little at the supper. She decided to go down to the kitchen and find something to eat rather than summon some sleepy half-dressed servant to attend her.

When she passed the drawing room, she noticed with primmed lips that the door was closed. From behind it came a murmur of voices. Her footsteps faltered, longing to listen at the door, but she went on down the stairs.

She cut herself a slice of game pie in the kitchen, drew a tankard of beer, and sat down at the scrubbed kitchen table and slowly ate and drank.

Lady Dacey was irritated with the duke. There was no sign of the flirtatious man of earlier in the evening. Instead he had given her a jaw-me-dead about the responsibility of bringing out a young girl and subjecting her to the iniquitous attentions of Lord Herne.

By the time he rose to take his leave, she was actually glad to see him go and remained sitting by the fire as he made his way out.

The duke descended the curved staircase to the hall. He had just reached the bottom step when Honoria emerged from the backstairs. She stopped at the sight of him.

She was still in her opera gown, one of those cunningly designed white dresses, heavily encrusted with embroidery, which revealed the excellence of her figure. She had removed her headdress and her brown hair curled delicately about her face and her blue eyes looked almost black.

He could not remember afterward approaching her, but suddenly he was standing next to her and the smell of her perfume was in his nostrils. They looked at each other in silence, both formal in evening dress, the duke in black coat and knee breeches, with a large diamond glittering in his cravat. He put his hands on either side of her face and bent his mouth to hers. Slowly they kissed, softly and intensely, lips only moving slightly against lips, body pressed to body, sweet emotions mingling, burning, feeling rising passion. He finally released her and said in a husky voice, 'We must talk, but not now, not here.' He heard a movement from upstairs. 'Tell Lady Dacey I shall call tomorrow at five to take you driving. Goodnight ... Honoria.'

He left abruptly. She heard the street door slam. She stood there for a few moments, one hand to her lips, wondering at the sudden rush of gladness, of *safeness*. Then she walked slowly up the stairs.

Lady Dacey emerged from the drawing room. She stopped short at the sight of Honoria. 'Was that Ware leaving?' she asked. 'Did you meet him?'

'Yes, Clarissa. He asked me to tell you he will be calling at five tomorrow to take me driving.'

'Oh, he did, did he? And what were you doing at this time of the day lurking about the hall waiting for him?'

'I happened to meet him when I was returning from the kitchen. I felt hungry and went to get something to eat.'

Lady Dacey gave her a long slow look and then retreated into the drawing room and slammed the door.

* * *

When the duke returned to his own home, he found a letter waiting for him from Mr Delaney. He read it with dismay and surprise. In it Mr Delaney said he had borne enough. He was riding north to see 'that vicar' and to ask him to release his wife.

'The mad Irish,' murmured the duke to himself.

Mr Delaney said that Mrs Perryworth was only to be told that he respected her wishes to end their friendship and that he had left Town.

The duke put aside the letter and then began

to wonder what to do about Honoria. Before he proposed marriage to her, he must find out if her feelings matched his own. She had let him kiss her. Surely she had responded. But he had been so carried away by the tide of his own passion that now he was not sure if she had reciprocated.

He could barely sleep, although it was dawn when he went to bed. He found the day went so slowly that he could hardly wait for five o'clock to arrive to see how she looked, how she behaved, if that kiss had meant as much to her as it had to him.

At precisely five he arrived at Hanover Square and was shown up to the drawing room. Lady Dacey did not like the Green Saloon favoured by Pamela and Honoria, simply because they preferred it.

The duke entered the drawing room. Lady Dacey was wearing a very dashing carriage dress of green velvet with gold frogs and epaulettes, and a bonnet decorated with cock's feathers on her head.

She smiled at him as radiantly as a young girl, holding out both hands to him in welcome. He kissed the air above both her hands and looked around. 'Where is Miss Goodham?'

'Honoria sends her apologies. That tiresome sister of Mrs Perryworth is ill again and has summoned her, and Honoria has gone too.'

His face was briefly a hard mask. 'But I would adore a drive,' said Lady Dacey brightly.

He was suddenly too weary and jaded to make any protest. 'Then I should be delighted to take you up,' he said.

* * *

Honoria sat in that darkened room in Lincoln's Inn Fields and listened with half an ear to the whining of the invalid. Amy had returned to her couch. Honoria had not told Pamela about that kiss, feeling it something too precious to share. She had woken later that morning after only a brief sleep, full of excitement and anticipation, thanking God that that most unlikely of men, the Duke of Ware, had fallen in love with her.

And then at two o'clock in the afternoon, Lady Dacey had entered her private sitting room, saying, 'Ware's servant has just called, Honoria. He says he is going to be too busy today to take you driving.'

Lady Dacey was just about to add that she wanted Honoria to do some shopping for her over at the mercer's on Ludgate Hill, so as to get the girl out of the house, when Pamela solved her problem by coming in at that moment to tell them that Amy had summoned her. Honoria said in a flat voice that she would go, too.

Both ladies listened to Amy and nursed their sore hearts. Pamela was trying not to think of

Mr Delaney and Honoria was trying to think of nothing at all.

* * *

Mrs Sarah Watkins was calling on the village gossip, Mrs Battersby, for tea.

She talked of this and that and then brought the conversation around to Mr Perryworth. 'He lives in such a simple style,' said Mrs Watkins. 'But vicars do have very little to live on.'

'Oh, he does that through choice, not necessity,' said Mrs Battersby. 'He has a good private income from a family trust. He is related to Sir Giles Perryworth of Harrogate, that family. He must have accumulated a fortune because he spends little on his household. His wife makes her own gowns, poor thing, and they have no children.'

Mrs Watkins, having gained the news she wanted, changed the topic. After she had left Mrs Battersby, she walked slowly along the village street, deep in thought. Such money as she had was coming to an end and she shuddered at the idea of the workhouse. She had shrewdly sensed that the vicar had never been in love and had laid her plans accordingly. Had it transpired that the vicar had very little money, then she would have needed to find someone else.

Her steps took her in the direction of the

vicarage. It was a dark windy day. She could see the oil lamp in the vicarage study burning brightly and the vicar bent over papers on his desk.

The vicar was writing to his wife, chiding her on the coldness of her letters, to ease his guilty conscience. Had he not met the delectable Mrs Watkins, he would have found nothing wrong with his wife's letters. Now he felt had Pamela been more affectionate, then he would not have found himself in this predicament, namely thinking of Mrs Watkins every minute of the day.

The study window was open at the top, the vicar being a great believer in fresh air, no matter what the weather. He heard a sharp cry, borne on the wind. Jumping to his feet he looked out of the window to see Mrs Watkins, her face distorted with pain, hanging onto the vicarage gate.

He ran out to her, crying, 'What ails you?'

'My ankle,' she said breathlessly. 'So silly of me. I twisted my ankle.'

'Come into the vicarage and let me have a look at it.' He put a strong arm about her and helped her along the path, glad that his cook-housekeeper had gone with the maid to the market in the neighbouring town.

He helped her into an armchair in the parlour, stirred up the fire, and rushed to close the window, an act that would have surprised Pamela, who had long ago come to the conclusion that her husband thought that coldness was next to godliness.

He knelt down in front of the window as she raised her skirt to expose one neat ankle. 'It doesn't seem swollen,' he said.

'These things always swell up later,' she said. He looked up at her. Her eyes began to glow. He was conscious of the emptiness of the house, of the wind howling in the chimney, of that coarse air of sensuality about her which stirred him so violently. He could not remove his gaze. He seemed to be trapped by her eyes. She gave a little sigh and moistened her lips with her tongue. Then all hell broke loose in Mr Perryworth and he half crouched over her, kissing and kissing those full lips, lost to the world and reason.

CHAPTER EIGHT

The Season had begun.

Honoria and Pamela were both listless in contrast to Lady Dacey, who sparkled and shone in the latest of new gowns. They went to balls, parties and routs, to turtle dinners and picnics, and at several of these events, Honoria could see the tall figure of the Duke of Ware, but not once did he come near her or ask her to dance.

She was wretchedly hurt and ashamed. That

kiss, which had seemed so wonderful and romantic, now appeared a dark and shameful thing, a practised rake amusing himself at the expense of an innocent. She and Pamela returned to their prayers, foreswore their novels, and yet did not talk to each other about their sorrows. Honoria was too ashamed of being 'tricked' by the duke, and Pamela felt she should not be breaking her heart over Mr Delaney, whom, she felt, might have written to her before leaving Town.

Outwardly, they were both very fashionable ladies, now well versed in all the rigid customs of that strange tribe called society. Honoria entertained young men, accepting bouquets, poems and compliments with aplomb, although Pamela often wondered if she actually ever *saw* any of her suitors. Lord Herne was in constant attendance and Lady Dacey turned a deaf ear to Pamela's complaints, saying that Herne was 'an old friend.'

Lady Dacey became more and more flirtatious with the duke, who seemed neither to encourage her or repel her. Into tolerance, she read smouldering passion held in check. She had become accustomed to her new 'respectable' appearance and already saw herself as the Duchess of Ware.

And then one day Lord Herne called and asked to see her privately. Knowing that Pamela and Honoria had gone to Lincoln's Inn

Fields and that therefore she was in no danger of being disturbed, she settled down with interest to listen to what he had to say.

'I have come to a decision about Miss Goodham,' he began. 'But first I would like to show you something.' He brought out of his pocket a heavy morocco box and flipped back the lid. A huge diamond blazed up from its bed of white satin. Lady Dacey drew a long, slow breath and one hand reached out for the gem. He snapped the lid shut. 'Not yet,' he said. 'You must order Miss Goodham to marry me.'

'She is a very strong-willed young miss. She will glare at me and pack her bags.'

He gave her a slow smile. 'No, she won't. Not if she does not have a home to go back to.'

'What can you mean?'

'I do not wish to sound conceited, but the facts are these. Ware is no longer interested in her, if he ever was. I am a catch. I have both title and fortune. I confess my reputation is a tiny bit black . . . gossip, my dear, only gossip. But the fact remains that while you were in Paris, Miss Goodham's name was linked with that of Ware in the social columns—Ware who is a notorious rake. But no parents came hot-footing it down from Yorkshire to protect their ewe lamb. So if you wish to earn this jewel, and I do mean earn, you will write to Mr and Mrs Goodham describing me in glowing terms and say that you wish to give me their permission to pay my addresses. Suggest that Miss Goodham might prove a bit flighty and missish and therefore it would be politic in them to *order* their daughter to marry me.'

'I have not seen my sister this age,' said Lady Dacey, inelegantly biting her thumb. 'She was always a tiny bit puritanical.'

He looked at her for a long moment and then said softly, 'And yet why do you think she allowed her daughter to be brought out by you?'

'No doubt because I have a title now. No one is puritanical when it comes to titles.'

'So, you see...?'

'Very well,' said Lady Dacey. 'I'll do it. But before I approach Honoria, I'll get her parents' permission. Why have you suddenly decided on marriage after all this time? To be frank, Honoria will sermonize you to death.'

'There is no other way I can have her,' he said brutally. He stood up and collected his hat and cane. 'Do not fail me,' he said, looking down at her. 'I make a bad enemy.'

'What is this talk of enemies?' Lady Dacey looked at him in surprise. 'If by any chance her parents refuse their permission, that is that.'

His eyes glowed with an evil light. His voice was silky. 'See that they do not.'

Lady Dacey sat nervously for some time after he had left. What could he do to her? His threats were surely empty. Then with a little sigh, she crossed the room to the writing desk and began to write to the Goodhams.

* * *

The duke was beginning to wonder why he stayed on in London. The cares of his estates beckoned. Lord Herne always seemed to be with Lady Dacey's party, and Honoria was obviously doing nothing to disaffect him. His rage at her had died and he wished it were back again, for now the sight of her, seemingly indifferent to his presence at balls and parties, gave him a dull ache. He was thoroughly ashamed of himself for having let himself get into such a miserable state over a young miss. London was surely full of fascinating beauties and yet he could not seem to find any. His secretary had done some research on the Goodham family for him. Apart from the disgraceful Lady Dacey, they seemed to have no other skeletons in their closet. They were an undistinguished gentry family, living in a quiet and religious way in Yorkshire. As a duke, he should be thinking of marrying someone of his own rank. He told himself it was ridiculous he should ever have contemplated proposing marriage to Honoria and tried to put her out of his mind. And yet he stayed in London.

For her part, Honoria felt she had sunk into a sort of numb state where nothing much seemed to matter. This wonderful London Season should be the highlight of her life. She should be treasuring memories of it for her future.

But she was shocked out of lethargy one day when Pamela said to her, 'I fear Lord Herne is going to ask both Lady Dacey and your parents for permission to marry you.'

'Let him ask,' said Honoria dully. 'I will not marry him.'

Pamela looked at her impatiently. 'You may have no option. If your parents and Lady Dacey give their permission, you will have no say in the matter. They were prepared to force you to marry Mr Pomfret. Had you encouraged the attentions of some other suitable man, then you would not be in this position.'

'But what can I do?' asked Honoria.

'It may not be too late,' urged Pamela. 'Look, let us sit down and write out a list of the young men I have noticed paying you court. We are going to the Palfreys' masked ball tonight. I suggest you begin to encourage someone more suitable.'

She sat down and began to write. 'You can score out Archie Buchan's name,' said Honoria, looking over her shoulder. 'And how many of the others think I am an heiress?'

'I wish the Duke of Ware had not decided to be so malicious,' sighed Pamela. 'Does he never approach you or speak to you?'

'No,' said Honoria bitterly. 'He is not worth troubling about, Pamela. He is a hardened rake.'

Pamela looked up at her. 'I never

understood what happened there, Honoria. Despite his reputation, I thought he behaved most kindly to you. In fact, I was ready to swear there was more than that.'

A slow, painful blush mounted to Honoria's cheeks and she turned her face away.

Pamela stood up and faced her. 'What is this? What happened? You must tell me. I am responsible for your welfare.'

Honoria hung her head and said on a little sigh, 'He kissed me.'

'Where?'

'On the mouth.'

'You widgeon! I mean, when?'

'It was the night you told Mr Delaney you did not want to see him again. Do you remember?'

'As if I could ever forget!'

'We came back here and Aunt asked Ware into the house and told both of us to go to bed.'

'I remember.'

'Well, I . . . I found I was hungry, for I had eaten practically nothing, and so I went down to the kitchen and had something, pie, I think. When I came back up to the hall, Ware was just leaving. He came up to me and kissed me. I thought he loved me, because of that kiss. He said he would call to take me driving the following afternoon. But he sent word that he was otherwise engaged and since then he has avoided me. That was the first kiss I had ever received, but for him, simply one of a thousand.'

'Oh, my dear, how very sad. You must put him out of your mind.'

'How I wish we did not have to go to this ball tonight!' exclaimed Honoria. 'How I long for one quiet evening at home. How I long to be able to rise and see the dawn instead of going to bed as the day breaks.'

'I confess to feeling very weary myself,' said Pamela. 'But Lady Dacey seems indefatigable. She has hopes of Ware, you know.'

Honoria winced. 'They are well suited.'

'I cannot believe that. Well, we may as well brace ourselves for another evening. At least we will be masked and so can scowl and look weary as much as we like.'

When Honoria had left, Pamela sat very still, feeling a great weight of sadness come over her. She wondered where Mr Delaney was. She suddenly wished she had not ended their friendship, that he were still in London, for he would know why Ware had behaved in such a cavalier way. It was surely not in Ware's character to kiss a young girl. Pamela then thought of Lord Herne and shuddered. She hated the way he looked at Honoria, the way his eyes fastened on her body. If only Ware . . . She bit the end of her quill pen and stared into space. Ware. There was one way to find out. He would surely be at the ball that evening. Why did she not seek him out and ask him? She began to brighten. As Honoria's chaperon it was her duty to ask him. Time, she felt, was running out for Honoria. Either she would find herself wed to Herne or return home in disgrace and be forced to wed Mr Pomfret. It was then she realized that the weekly letter from her husband had not arrived. Perhaps the weather had been bad in the north and the mail delayed. She bent her head to the task of listing Honoria's suitors.

* * *

Mr Sean Delaney put up at an inn in the largest town near to the village where the Perryworths lived. Now that he was actually in Yorkshire, he felt his courage waning. The vicar would be outraged. He would tell Honoria's parents, who would be alarmed that their daughter's chaperon had been behaving so disgracefully. But he had come this far and he was determined not to turn back. In all his feckless idle life, he had never been more determined on anything.

The weather on the following day boosted his spirits. It was warm and sunny with great fleecy clouds chasing each other across the sky.

He saw the spire of the church rising above the fields. The vicarage, he knew, would be hard by the church. He found it easily enough and dismounted and tethered his horse to the gate post. As he approached the vicarage, he sensed that no one was at home. No smoke rose from the chimney. All was still and quiet. He knocked loudly, waited and listened, but no one answered.

He walked over to the church and pushed open the door. The interior was dim and the old flagstones on the aisle were splashed with rectangles of blue and red and gold from the stained glass windows. To his right, a marble tomb gleamed whitely, two angels holding laurel wreaths up to the hammerbeam ceiling. He was about to turn away when a movement from the altar caught his eye. He walked forward. A village woman was polishing the brass rail.

'Good morning,' said Mr Delaney. 'Would you be so good as to tell me where I can find Mr Perryworth?'

The woman bobbed a curtsy and then said, 'Him's gone.'

'Gone? Where?'

'Squire says him's gone to visit a relative in Leicester.'

Mr Delaney stood there feeling helpless.

'When does he return?'

'Don't know, sir, I'm sure.'

Mr Delaney turned and left the church and stood outside in the sunshine. Then he began to walk forward slowly to the vicarage again. He wanted to see where she lived, to imagine her sitting in those rooms. Feeling guilty, he looked about him, but no one was in sight. He looked in one window: a rather bleak parlour with a sanded floor and a mudcoloured rug, heavy old-fashioned furniture, a bookcase with what looked like heavy ecclesiastical tomes, a stone fireplace, and a square table. It appeared, he thought, as if no one had ever lived there. He glanced over his shoulder again and then moved to the next window. This was obviously the vicar's study: a desk with an oil lamp, bookshelves, pens and ink, and on the desk, two letters, both sealed.

He leaned closer. The sun was behind him and a shaft of sunlight struck the letters on the desk. One, he read, was addressed to the bishop and the other to Pamela. His heart beat hard. Why should the vicar leave a letter to his wife on his desk instead of sending it when she was not due to return from London for some time? All at once, he was desperate to know what was in that letter to Pamela. He walked round the house, looking for a way in, but every window was closed and every door locked.

At first he thought he would return to the inn and wait until night fell, then return and break a window. But perhaps the safer option would be to visit this squire and find out if there were any rumours that the vicar had fled.

The squire, he learned from a shop in the village that appeared to sell everything from candles to corsets, was Sir John Cartwright and he lived in the manor house just outside the village. Mr Delaney rode there, hoping that the squire would be at home.

Sir John was pleased to receive him. He was a dingy, gross sort of man, slouched in his study, surrounded by dogs. A female voice could be heard berating a servant somewhere else in the house, showing that there was probably a Lady Cartwright.

'Sit down,' said Sir John. 'We are glad to receive a gentleman. Not many of them around here.'

Mr Delaney sat opposite him and accepted a glass of white brandy, which he shrewdly guessed had been smuggled. The squire heaved himself out of his chair and stirred up the fire with his boot and then sank back again with a grunt. 'What brings you here?' he asked.

'I came to find Mr Perryworth, your vicar.'

'He has gone to visit relatives, I believe,' said the squire.

'I looked in at the window of his study,' said Mr Delaney, adding hurriedly, 'just to make sure no one was at home. There are two letters on his desk, one to the bishop and the other to Mrs Perryworth.'

'So?' The squire raised his bushy eyebrows. 'Why shouldn't a man leave letters in his own house and on his own desk?'

'As Mrs Perryworth is chaperoning Miss Goodham at the London Season, which still has some length of time to run, why did he not post it?'

'Forgot?'

'But neither letter is *addressed.* It is as if they have been left there to be found at a later date.'

'The vicar probably wrote both letters, then was in a rush to go and see his relatives, and so forgot to address them and post them.' The squire looked smug in a patronizing way.

'In any case,' said Mr Delaney, cursing this stupid squire in his heart, 'I shall be returning to London. Is there one of the vicar's servants in the village who could get me that letter for Mrs Perryworth so that I can deliver it?'

'There's Mrs Jones, the cook-housekeeper.'

'Then she must go daily to clean, if she does not live in.'

'She lives there when the Perryworths are in residence, but the vicar said he did not want the house to be disturbed and paid her for a month, so she is residing with her sister over at Lower End.'

'Which is where?'

'Five miles out on the east road.'

Mr Delaney forced himself to stay where he was and engage the squire in conversation for another quarter of an hour before making his escape. He rode out on the east road until he reached Lower End, which was an indistinguished hamlet without shop or church or inn. He soon found Mrs Jones, a sturdy Welshwoman, who listened carefully. Then it was as if a shutter had closed down over her eyes.

'The reason I am come to you,' pursued Mr

Delaney, 'is because I shall see Mrs Perryworth in London and I could take her that letter.'

'Reckon it's nobody's business but vicar's,' said Mrs Jones, folding sturdy red shiny arms like potted meat. He felt like shaking her. He suddenly decided to return to his original plan and go back after dark and break into the vicarage.

But he had one last try. 'Let me put it to you like this, Mrs Jones. A man who leaves letters for his wife and his bishop on his desk and disappears usually is a man who has taken his own life.'

'Vicar'd never do that!' exclaimed Mrs Jones. 'Not over that whore.'

'What whore?' asked Mr Delaney.

She stood for a long time in silence, staring at her square-buckled shoes. He made an impatient noise and turned toward his horse.

'Wait, sir!' she cried. She put a large hand into her apron pocket and produced a key. 'This fits the lock in the back door.'

Mr Delaney seized it and mounted and rode off before she could change her mind.

When he reached the vicarage, he saw to his irritation that there was a light gig drawn up outside and the squire and a thin angular lady were peering in the study window. As he approached them, he heard the lady say, 'You always were a fool. Never could see what was happening under your nose, you were so busy ogling her yourself.'

Mr Delaney coughed and they swung round. The squire introduced his wife. 'I have the key to the back door,' said Mr Delaney firmly, 'and I consider it my duty as a friend of Mrs Perryworth to see what is in that letter.'

'You cannot go opening a letter that is not addressed to you,' protested the squire.

'If he doesn't, I will,' said Lucy Cartwright, giving her husband an impatient push.

They walked round to the back of the house and Mr Delaney turned the key in the lock and walked inside. The squire and his wife followed. The chill and the dreariness of the house struck Mr Delaney. Even if the vicar turned out to have behaved in a respectable way and had merely gone to visit relatives as he had said, Mr Delaney was determined Pamela should never return to this house.

They went into the study. Despite a short bark of protest from the squire, Mr Delaney picked up the letter with Pamela's name on it, broke the seal, and carried it to the window.

He scanned the contents and then read them very slowly and carefully. In stilted language, the vicar informed his wife he had gone to America to start a new life. He said that as their marriage had never been consummated, he could no longer regard them as man and wife. To that end, he had written to the bishop asking for an annulment.

'Well, what does it say?' demanded Lady Cartwright impatiently.

Mr Delaney handed her the letter. She fumbled in her bosom for her quizzing glass and then read it avidly. 'It is as I thought,' she exclaimed. 'He has run off with Mrs Watkins.'

'What!' yelled the squire.

'He says nothing about a Mrs Watkins in the letter,' pointed out Mr Delaney.

'Oh, we all knew what was going on,' said Lady Cartwright, 'all of us with the exception of this fool of a husband of mine and that idiot, Pomfret, whom she was chasing after in case she did not bring the vicar up to the mark.'

'I cannot believe any of this,' protested the squire.

'Then where is Mrs Watkins? Mrs Battersby said she left the same day as the vicar.'

The squire sighed. He picked up the bishop's letter. 'I will send my man over to the bishop with this. We must ride after them and bring them back.'

Lady Cartwright snorted with contempt. 'They left over a week ago. And would you have him dragged back in disgrace? He will be excommunicated, and then what will be left to him but to make that pretty wife of his more miserable than ever?'

Mr Delaney twitched the letter to Pamela out of her hands. 'I must be on my way.' His face was radiant. 'Have no fear, this will be delivered personally to Mrs Perryworth.'

* * *

Pamela, Honoria, and Lady Dacey set out that night for the ball. Honoria was wearing a blue velvet mask and was glad of its protection against the burning gaze of Lord Herne who was, as usual, accompanying them. Honoria was weary of this London marriage market game. How terrible to be forced into finding a husband, any husband other than Lord Herne. Beside her, Pamela quietly hoped that the duke would be there, wondering at the same time how she would find an opportunity to approach him, for he never asked her to dance or approached her either. Then an idea occurred to her and she quickly bent and ripped the hem of her gown.

They were late as usual, Lady Dacey liking to make an entrance. She had reverted to one of her scandalous gowns, transparent muslin worn over flesh-coloured stockings and a corset, and the bumps and ridges of her corset could be clearly seen through her filmy gown. How such a sight was supposed to attract any man was a wonder, thought Honoria, noticing that the red wig was also once more in place. She had lectured her aunt on the virtues of modesty and Lady Dacey had appeared to have listened to her, but, Honoria realized sadly, had not been taking in a word of it. The fact was that Lady Dacey had noticed that Ware no longer complimented her on her gowns and put it down to her new 'dowdy' appearance. Her eyes glittered behind her mask with anticipation. This, she was determined, would be the night when she brought him up to the mark.

It was a perfect evening, warm enough at last to make the ladies feel comfortable in their fashionably thin gowns. The Palfreys had a large mansion. All the curtains were drawn back and, as they arrived, they could see masked dancers moving through the brightly lit rooms.

They left their cloaks in an anteroom. 'Coming, Pamela?' demanded Lady Dacey impatiently from the doorway.

'Go on ahead,' said Pamela. 'My hem is coming down. I will mend it and follow you.'

'We will wait for you,' said Honoria.

'Fiddle,' exclaimed Lady Dacey, anxious to make her appearance.

'It is all right, Honoria,' urged Pamela. 'I shall be some time.'

Honoria left reluctantly with her aunt. Pamela took a small box of sewing materials out of her reticule and stitched diligently at the hem. But when it was repaired, she continued to sit there. She planned to enter the ballroom between dances, boldly approach the Duke of Ware and ask him why he had kissed Honoria and then refused to have anything to do with her again.

A country dance had just started. Fortunately there was a clock on the mantelpiece in the anteroom. The dance would last a good half an hour. She settled down to wait.

* * *

The Duke of Ware had almost decided not to go. He had written to his agent to say that he would be returning to his estates. Most of the servants had been sent on. He planned to spend his last evening in London quietly in his town house. But as evening approached and he could hear through the open windows the bustle of London coming awake for the pleasures of the night, he was seized with an aching restlessness. *She* would be there, cool and indifferent to his presence as usual. But surely it was his duty to give her one last severe warning against Herne. And so he persuaded himself that he must go. He summoned his valet and said he had changed his mind and wished his evening dress to be laid out. He reached the Palfreys' without much difficulty for most of the guests had already arrived, and so he did not have to wait in the usual queue of carriages to be put down.

He entered the hall and handed his cloak, hat, and stick to a footman and walked toward the stairs.

'Your Grace?'

A timid female voice hailed him and he swung round.

Pamela had hardly been able to believe her

luck when she had finally left the anteroom to see the duke just arriving. And yet it had taken a lot of courage to hail him.

He was wearing a black velvet mask but Pamela knew she would recognize those odd tawny eyes of his anywhere. He bowed and waited, emanating an arrogant, frosty chill.

Pamela's courage almost deserted her. She firmly reminded herself of her duties as chaperon. She rose from a low curtsy and faced him determinedly. 'I would have a word in private with you, Your Grace, about Honoria—about Miss Goodham.'

His eyebrows rose superciliously but he said, 'Go on.'

A party of late arrivals chattered in the doorway. Pamela spread her hands in a helpless gesture. 'Not here.'

He summoned a footman. 'I wish a few words in private with Mrs Perryworth.' The footman, used to the intrigues of the quality, led them to a door off the hall and threw it open.

'Leave the door open,' said Pamela, aware of the curious stares of the arriving guests.

It was a little-used saloon, little-used to judge by the stale, cold smell of the air.

'Now, Mrs Perryworth,' said the duke haughtily, 'explain yourself.' He spoke to Pamela as if addressing her over a wide social gulf.

'Your Grace,' began Pamela, unable to meet

his eyes but addressing a dusty vase of blue john instead, 'I have heard something from Honoria this very day which prompts me, as her chaperon, to ask you your intentions.'

The surprise in his eyes was so great that she coloured, thinking for one awful moment that Honoria had made the whole thing up.

'My intentions? What intentions, pray?'

'I must make myself plain. Oh, dear. How distasteful and embarrassing all this is. I only learned this very day that you kissed Miss Goodham and made arrangements to take her driving the following day. Then you cancelled that arrangement and have cut her quite dreadfully since. I know something of your reputation, Your Grace, and yet I cannot quite believe such bad behaviour.'

'Mrs Perryworth, I assure you, I called as arranged to take Miss Goodham driving and was told by Lady Dacey that you had both gone off to visit your sister in Lincoln's Inn Fields. I was then somehow constrained to take Lady Dacey driving.'

Pamela shook her head in bewilderment. 'Why did you not tell her this? Do you not see, Your Grace, she damns you as a heartless philanderer? Lady Dacey lied to us.'

He felt suddenly, ridiculously, lighthearted. 'I will put matters right directly, Mrs Perryworth. I thank you. I am cursed with a stubborn pride. Your arm, ma'am. Let us find Miss Goodham.'

They left the room together and began to mount the staircase just as Honoria appeared at the head of it. She had noticed Pamela's long absence, had become worried, and had just started to go in search of her. She stopped short at the sight of Pamela on the arm of the duke and would have turned on her heel had not Pamela called to her, 'Stay, Honoria. His Grace has something to say to you.'

They came up to her. 'I will talk further to you later, Mrs Perryworth,' said the duke. 'Miss Goodham, I wish to speak to you in private.' Pamela curtsied to him and released his arm. Honoria looked wide-eyed at Pamela, who gave a little nod. She looked up at the duke in a dazed way. He was smiling down at her. He held out his arm. In a dream she placed her fingertips on the silk sleeve of his coat as he led her back down the stairs. Some ladies were leaving the anteroom. She was only dimly conscious of their faces staring upward, of their high voices.

The footman who had ushered the duke and Pamela into the saloon off the hall now sprang to open the door again, giving a surreptitious wink to his colleagues as he did so. The Duke of Ware was living up to his reputation, particularly when he firmly shut the door this time on the watching footmen. He removed his mask and tucked it into his pocket.

'Honoria,' he said. 'Why did you not ask me why I had not come to take you driving? I did come. But the intriguing Lady Dacey told me that you had left to visit Mrs Perryworth's sister. I felt cut and snubbed.'

'But . . . but Aunt Clarissa told me you had sent a messenger to say that you were too busy. Why did you not say anything to me?'

'Because I thought one kiss that had meant so much to me meant nothing to you.'

'How could you think that?' cried Honoria, shocked into bluntness. 'It was a first kiss for me, but only one of a thousand for you.'

'But the only one that ever mattered.' He reached out and untied the strings of her mask. She blushed and looked down.

He took her face between his hands. 'Will you marry me, Honoria?'

She raised her eyes to his and said simply, 'Yes.'

He bent his mouth to hers and this time kissed her and kissed her again, each kiss hungrier than the last, each kiss making up for time wasted. At last she drew back a little and looked up at him anxiously. 'Your mistress . . .?' she whispered.

'That is long over. There is no other woman for me now. I want you, Honoria. I want you completely.'

And that seemed not at all scandalous to Honoria, but a very right and proper statement, and so she wound her arms round his neck and buried her fingers in his hair and kissed him so passionately that he eventually put her away from him and began to talk rapidly and breathlessly of how soon he could get a special licence.

Pamela had refused to dance. She was sitting with the other chaperons, her chair facing across the ballroom where she could command a view of the entrance through the shifting, turning dancers. And then just as a dance ended, she saw them. They were both masked again but they exuded happiness. She gave a choked little sigh of relief and then was overcome with such a sharp longing for Mr Delaney that she nearly cried out.

The duke had no intention of waiting until the ball was over to ask Lady Dacey's permission to marry Honoria. Lady Dacey was delighted when he said he wanted a few words with her. She rolled her huge eyes in a languishing way at him as he led her out of the ballroom. The waiting footmen in the hall exchanged glances as the duke descended the stairs with yet another lady.

But this time he left the door open. 'Lady Dacey,' he began, and then took a step backward, for she was almost leaning up against him, 'I wish to pay my addresses to your niece. I wish to marry her.'

Lady Dacey stared at him, amazed. 'You can't,' she said finally.

His brows snapped together. 'Why not?'

'Honoria is promised to Lord Herne.'

'Does she know this?'

'N-no. I wrote to her parents and asked their permission.'

'Honoria wishes to marry me. I wish to marry her. That is all you need to know. You will tell Herne that his suit is no longer welcome.'

Lady Dacey bit her thumb in that nervous way she had when she was upset. She felt miserable. She felt sure the scheming Honoria had stolen this duke away from her. And Herne would be nasty. Still, what could he do, and what could she do? Honoria's parents would naturally prefer a duke for their daughter.

'Very well. I'll speak to Herne,' she said. She thought of that diamond, and sighed bitterly.

CHAPTER NINE

Honoria and Pamela had retired to bed. The Duke of Ware had left. Lord Herne and Lady Dacey sat facing each other.

'I am most displeased with you,' said Lord Herne.

Lady Dacey gave a little shrug. 'What else could I do? They both want each other. Surely you could see that.'

'I warned you. I make a bad enemy. But you can still do something for me. Tomorrow, I want you to send the servants away by four in the afternoon. You will also send Mrs Perryworth off on some errand and you will drug Honoria and then leave her to me. I will have her first and if Ware wants my leavings, it is then up to him.'

'He will kill you!'

'I will be out of the country.'

'No, of course, I would not dream of doing such a dreadful thing. Why should I?'

'Because, my dear, if you do not, I shall expose you.'

'What are you talking about?' Lady Dacey's voice was shrill.

'I called one day when you were out. To pass the time until your return, I picked the lock of your desk and read your correspondence.' Lady Dacey turned a muddy colour under her paint.

'Oh, yes. Everyone believes you and Dacey were man and wife, but that was not the case. You returned from Italy and put it about that you were wed there. So I was most interested to read a letter from an old servant in Italy who was dying and who appeared very fond of you, begging you to legalize your position. Old Dacey was senile when he died and really believed you were man and wife and so left everything to you. But I could have it all taken away from you.'

'I shall burn that letter!'

'Which you should have done a long time ago. But all I have to do is approach your peers and suggest an investigation. You would be asked for proof, for the name of who married you and where. The only way you can stop my mouth is doing what I ask.'

'But Ware will kill *me*!'

'He will think I drugged her. I shall return here at four o'clock. Let me in and make yourself scarce. Sleep on it. You will see it is the only way. I suggest you have her drugged by three in the afternoon. That way she will be ready for me.'

Pamela was surprised to be summoned by Lady Dacey as early as noon and given a list of shopping to do and told not to return until she had completed it . . . surprised because Lady Dacey hardly ever rose until two in the afternoon and because, like most ladies, when not amusing herself by shopping, she sent her servants or summoned the tradespeople to the house.

She was further bewildered when told by one of the maids that Lady Dacey had ordered all servants to leave the house that afternoon and not to return until after dark. When she asked Lady Dacey about this, an unusually haggard Lady Dacey replied that 'the poor things' deserved some time to themselves. This, thought Pamela, from a woman who never seemed to notice that her servants were human beings.

When she suggested that Honoria might accompany her on this prolonged shopping expedition, Lady Dacey turned pale and said in a low voice that she and Honoria would take the opportunity to discuss the wedding arrangements.

'What is wrong with her?' asked Pamela. 'I know she is very upset because she thought for some reason that Ware wanted her.'

'But if she wishes to discuss wedding arrangements,' said Honoria, 'then she certainly must have accepted the engagement. But how very odd!'

Honoria became more bewildered when she was finally seated with Lady Dacey over the tea tray in the drawing room that afternoon. Pamela and the servants had left and Lady Dacey herself had carried the tea things up from the kitchen. From time to time, someone hammered at the door, but Lady Dacey said, 'We do not want to be troubled with callers.'

'But Ware will be calling,' protested Honoria. 'That last caller might have been him!'

'Oh, you will be seeing him for the rest of your life.' Lady Dacey's large eyes shone with tears. 'We will settle down and have tea and a comfortable coze.'

Honoria rose and went to the window. The day was dark and rainy. Rain drummed down on the cobbles but the square below was deserted except for a crossing sweeper at the corner and a closed carriage rattling over the cobbles. This she could see by cupping her hands on either side of her face, for the room behind her was brightly lit with many candles. And then as she stood back from the window, it became a mirror caused by the darkness of the day outside. She could see the room behind her reflected in the glass. Just before she turned round, she saw Lady Dacey take a little phial and empty the contents into the cup which had been set at her place.

Honoria's heart began to thud. The most sensible thing surely would be to confront her aunt and demand to know what she had poured into that cup. On the other hand, she had to know Lady Dacey's plan, for if this one was thwarted, there would be another attempt. She walked back and sat down.

'Now drink your tea while it is hot,' commanded Lady Dacey.

Honoria stared over her shoulder at the door and exclaimed, 'What is that?'

Lady Dacey started up and looked around. Honoria quickly poured half the contents of her cup onto the thick carpet under the table. When her aunt said, 'Nothing. Nobody there, you silly goose,' and turned back, Honoria was lowering a cup now half full of liquid from her lips as if she had already drunk it.

'Well, Aunt . . . I mean, Clarissa . . . I gather you wish to discuss wedding arrangements with me.'

'Indeed, yes, but I fear you have been roused too early, Honoria. You look so very tired.

Would you not like to lie down for a little?'

Drugged, not poisoned, thought Honoria. Thank God for small mercies. She drooped her eyelids and said faintly, 'I am indeed very tired. Perhap if you will excuse me . . .'

'Let me help you.' Lady Dacey stood up at the same time as Honoria and put an arm about her waist. Despite her worry and fear, Honoria could not help wishing, and not for the first time either, that her aunt would try bathing instead of dowsing her body with scent instead. But she suffered herself to be led to her bedroom. 'I will just lie on the top of the bed,' she said faintly. She lay back and closed her eyes. Honoria suddenly felt she knew why her aunt was doing this and began to feel amused. She felt she knew the reason for the dismissal of the servants, although why her aunt had not thought to send her away with Pamela was a puzzle. Of course it must be that Lady Dacey was about to receive a lover.

Her aunt's initial feeling of relief was short lived. On a table beside Honoria's bed was Lady Dacey's own Bible, a great brassbound tome that Honoria had borrowed. Lady Dacey looked from Honoria's beautiful face to the Bible and back again. She drew up a chair beside the bed and waited.

* * *

Pamela was working her way through the

shopping list, her temper rising. Although she did not have to carry anything because she had asked the tradespeople to deliver the goods on the morrow, rain was beginning to drip down her neck despite the calash she wore over her bonnet, her skirts were muddy, and as she was wearing pattens over her shoes, she was always worried that the high ring of iron on the soles would cause her to twist an ankle on the cobbles. She was walking along Pall Mall when she heard herself hailed from a carriage and looked up into the features of the Duke of Ware.

'Why are you alone and unescorted?' he asked, jumping down to join her.

'I think your engagement has overset my lady's wits,' said Pamela. 'She has given me a long list of shopping, the servants have been dismissed and told not to return until dark, and all because she wants to discuss wedding arrangements!'

'I called and there was no reply,' said the duke. 'What ails the woman? When did Herne leave last night?'

'I do not know. Honoria and I retired to bed and left him with Lady Dacey. As you know, he took your engagement badly, although he said nothing.'

'Get in my carriage,' he said abruptly. 'I do not like this.'

He helped Pamela up. She sat beside him in the open carriage, wondering why the gentlemen of the aristocracy appeared to favour open carriages in all weather.

They arrived at Hanover Square and the duke called to his tiger to go to the horses' heads, helped Pamela down, and ran to the door and hammered furiously on it with the gold knob of his ebony stick.

'No reply,' said Pamela helplessly. 'What are we to do?'

'This,' he said. He leaned across from the step and smashed at the windows of the Green Saloon with the knob of his stick. The noise was deafening. Shards of glass tumbled down into the area below. Heads popped out of windows of the adjoining houses. The duke climbed up onto the railings beside the door and stepped nimbly onto the window-sill and dived in through the shattered glass while Pamela stood shivering in the rain.

* * *

Ten minutes before this, Lady Dacey had let Lord Herne in and locked the door again behind him. 'You have done it?' he asked. 'She is ready?'

Lady Dacey nodded dully.

'Then lead the way.'

Lady Dacey walked slowly up the stairs. Why was she doing this? She could not get away with it. There would be questions and questions. Oh, what a coincidence, the duke would sneer, that Honoria was drugged and raped on the very day that Lady Dacey decided to dismiss the servants and send Mrs Perryworth away. And yet, the alternative was ruin and possibly the gallows for having dared to pretend to be a peeress.

Lord Herne walked past her and into Honoria's bedchamber. He stood at the end of the bed, rubbing his hands, like a gourmet about to embark on a delicious meal.

It was then that Honoria opened her eyes and saw him and knew why Lady Dacey had tried to drug her. She screamed.

He made a dive for her and Lady Dacey seized a vase from a stand outside the door and brought it down on Lord Herne's head.

'Curse you,' he shouted. 'I will expose you.' He reeled past her and out onto the landing. He leaned for a moment against the balustrade and shook his head as if to clear it.

Lady Dacey, sobbing, ran to the bedside and seized the Bible. She swung round and threw it as hard as she could. It sailed out through the door and caught Lord Herne on the side of the head as he leaned against the balustrade. He gave an odd sort of moan and before Honoria's horrified eyes, he toppled slowly over the edge and straight down to the marble tiles of the hall below.

The duke rushed into the hall from the Green Saloon just as Lord Herne struck the floor. He looked up. Lady Dacey and Honoria appeared far above, staring in horror. He bounded up the stairs and Honoria flew down them to meet him, crying, 'He was going to rape me!'

* * *

The hushing-up process of the death of Lord Herne seemed to take forever. The Duke of Ware had no desire to see a future in-law in the dock. The only thing Lady Dacey would not tell him was what hold Herne had over her to make her behave in such a disgraceful way.

The authorities were informed that Lord Herne had had a dizzy attack and had fallen to his death. Then, when they were alone, the duke asked Honoria why on earth she had gone along with the plan.

'I did not think of Herne,' said Honoria, still white and shaken. 'I wanted to see what she was up to. I thought that, as she had lost all hope of you, she planned to receive a lover. I thought I would pretend to be asleep and then, when the lover arrived, try to shock Aunt Clarissa into virtue.'

'You cannot stay here,' he said firmly. 'I will never trust that woman again.'

'We must forgive her,' said Honoria. 'She is so contrite and she did kill him in order to defend me. He did have some dreadful hold over her. She is kind and really good and would not have harmed me.'

'Where is Mrs Perryworth?'

'Pamela is in bed with a bad cold. In all the excitement, you forgot she was standing outside in the rain and she was left there for about an hour, explaining to the watch and curious servants from the houses next door that she had forgotten her key and that you had broken through the windows so as to let her in.'

'I could not inform the authorities until we all worked out how to hush things up, and so I did forget about poor Mrs Perryworth,' said the duke. 'But if Lady Dacey has some montrous sin in her past, so monstrous that it gave Herne a hold over her and she cannot bear to say what it is, then this is no place for you, my love.'

'There is good in everyone,' said Honoria firmly. Her eyes sparkled in her wan face. 'Even you.'

And that was enough to make him gather her in his arms and hold her close and kiss her fiercely, so fiercely that neither of them was aware that Lady Dacey had entered the room and was watching them.

She slowly backed out and went down the stairs and stood in the hall, staring down at the spot where Lord Herne's dead body had so recently lain. She was a murderess, she told herself, and a liar. She could not bear herself. She would go into a convent and become a nun and do good works for the rest of her life to atone for her sins. Overcome with the great burden of guilt, she sank to her knees to pray.

And then just before she closed her eyes, she saw something sparkle and glint in a far corner of the hall. She shuffled forward on her knees like a pilgrim to have a closer look.

On its side lay that morocco box, and a little way away, practically hidden by a fold in the long hall curtains, lay the diamond. It must have tumbled out of Lord Herne's pocket when he fell.

Her fingers closed over it. The wages of sin, said a voice in her head. She rose to her feet, still clutching the diamond. The fire from it seemed to warm her blood. She gave a little fatalistic shrug. It was always better to sleep on things. Always better to make decisions in the morning. So, holding the diamond tightly, she went upstairs to bed.

* * *

Pamela, although recovered from her cold, began to feel increasingly depressed. The sight of the duke and Honoria so dizzyingly in love reminded her of the bleak future that lay before her. Although her husband had ceased to write to her, she continued to send letters home.

Lady Dacey had taken to her bedchamber. She claimed she was ill and took all her meals in her room, and so it was left to Pamela to escort Honoria to balls and parties. Quite often now,

Pamela would refuse to dance. She would sit with the chaperons and watch the door and dream that one day Mr Delaney would come walking in and smile at her in that way of his that made her heart turn over.

Mr and Mrs Goodham had written to announce their imminent arrival. Pamela, sitting against the wall at yet another ball at the Buchans', knew they would probably arrive on the morrow. Should by any chance Mr Delaney come back to London, then she would not be able to talk to him or smile on him, for she knew Honoria's parents would report such behaviour to her husband. Her heart sank even lower. Possibly her husband had decided to travel south with them and that was the reason he had not written.

So she had one last ball where she could dream. She refused the first gentleman who asked her to dance and so was free to sit and dream for the rest of the ball. Her only comfort was in occasionally taking her eyes away from the entrance to watch the duke and Honoria waltzing together as if they were alone, as if no one else in the world mattered. The waltz came to an end. Honoria sank into a deep curtsy and smiled up at the duke, all the love in the world in her eyes. Pamela's own eyes blurred with tears and she looked toward the entrance again.

At first she thought it was a dream, as the figure of Mr Delaney, drowned in her tears, swam into her vision. She blinked the tears away and stared. And there he was, his eyes anxiously scanning the room. He saw her and his face lit up and he crossed quickly to her side.

'Oh, how very beautiful you are,' he sighed, and Pamela, who had been feeling up till that moment old and frumpy, glowed at him. 'Come with me,' he said. 'I have good news. I hope you will think it good news. Please.'

Pamela hesitated. 'Honoria's parents will be arriving soon and I must be careful. I must not be seen talking to you.'

'You will find that no longer matters. Come!'

Wondering, she went with him. He led her to the back of the ballroom and opened a French window. They found themselves on a terrace overlooking a moon-washed garden.

'Now,' he said, 'I have a letter for you. You won't be able to read it here, so I'll tell you about it.'

Pamela listened in amazement as he told her the contents of the letter and then went on to explain what it did not contain but what the whole of the village now knew, that the vicar had run off to America with Mrs Watkins.

'I can hardly believe it,' said Pamela. 'He is such a cold, unfeeling man, not given over to passion at all! And he wants an annulment!'

'Do you see what that means, my love? We are free.'

Pamela looked at him shyly. 'Do you mean...?'

He drew her to him. 'We will marry as soon as we can. I fell in love with you the evening I saw you drinking champagne at that inn.'

She leaned against him with a sigh. 'I have been so very lonely,' she said.

He kissed her until they both felt dizzy but they could not bear to be apart, and so they kept on kissing and caressing while the shadows of the dancers moved across the windows behind them, and on and on, until the sky began to pale and the first birdsong arose from the bushes in the garden.

* * *

Mr Perryworth lay in his berth on the *Mary Belle* as she ploughed her way across the Atlantic and wished he could die. He had suffered from seasickness since the day they had left port. At first Mrs Watkins had been solicitous, then bored, and on the few occasions when he had been able to drag himself up on deck it was to see her flirting boldly with the ship's captain. So he lay and suffered and thought of the times he had been ill in the past and Pamela had bathed his hot forehead and Pamela had read to him and Pamela had given him nourishing meals. Now he was bound for America and tied to a noisy jade. The more he thought of Mrs Watkins, the more repulsive she seemed, and he could no longer feel any of that mad passion which had driven him to take such a step. He had a shrewd idea that she was after his money and that had been his only attraction for her. It was she who had suggested he draw it all out of the bank and take it in gold sovereigns. The money was under his pillow.

All at once he decided that as soon as they landed, he would escape from her and start a new life on his own somewhere. America was a good place to hide, she had said. He smiled sourly to himself. Mrs Watkins would shortly find out for herself just how good a place it was!

* * *

Honoria's wedding to the duke was a very grand affair, although the gossips wagged their tongues and said it had been indecently rushed. An engagement of only three months!

During that three months Lady Dacey had kept to her room. Pamela and Mrs Goodham had made all the wedding arrangements with the help of the duke's secretary.

Lady Dacey finally roused herself to attend the wedding. She dressed soberly and wore a hat with a veil. The service was very moving and Honoria was described as the most beautiful bride ever. Lady Dacey cried noisily throughout the service and was still in tears at the wedding breakfast.

She was quite resolved that when the dancing started, she would retire to her room and was on the point of doing so when a gentleman's voice said, 'You must not be so distressed.'

She found she was being addressed by a middle-aged gentleman, Sir Frederick Tomkins, whom she remembered with an effort as being a relative on the duke's side of the family.

'The bride is your niece, I believe,' said Sir Frederick. 'You must be very fond of her.'

'I am crying because the minx stole Ware away from me,' said Lady Dacey waspishly.

'Now how could that happen?' he said gallantly. 'What man would set eyes on another after having seen you?'

She looked up at him. He had silver hair and bright blue eyes that held a wicked twinkle. Her large eyes began to sparkle.

'La, sir, you are only saying that.'

'Not I. When I saw your distress, I felt my heart break.'

'Tish, sir, you are like all gentlemen; you have no heart.'

'Not for anyone else, ma'am, only for you. I am sure your dancing equals your beauty.'

'Naughty man!' Lady Dacey giggled. 'Well, just one dance!'

* * *

'I think your aunt is a very wicked woman,' said the duke drowsily the following morning. 'I would dearly like to know what it is in her past that made her do such a dreadful thing for Lord Herne.'

'I do not know,' said Honoria. 'The only time before the wedding she roused herself to do anything was to burn masses of old letters and documents.'

'Perhaps she murdered someone else and he found out about it.'

'She did not murder Lord Herne. She only threw the Bible at him. It was an accident.'

'A lucky accident for her I am sure, or Herne would have betrayed her.'

'Sean Delaney has amazed me,' the duke went on. 'I have done everything that is in my power or my lawyers' power to help him. He is so amazingly patient waiting for the annulment to come through.'

'He is happy and so is Pamela,' said Honoria. 'It is now daylight and ... and I feel ... shy lying here naked. Do you mind if I put something on?'

'Not at all,' he said. 'Try this,' and he rolled his naked body on top of hers, and Honoria forgot about Pamela and Mr Delaney and wicked Lady Dacey for at least the next hour.

We hope you have enjoyed this Large Print book. Other Chivers Press or Thorndike Press Large Print books are available at your library or directly from the publishers. For more information about current and forthcoming titles, please call or write, without obligation, to: